THE WICKED WOLVES OF WOLVES WINDSOR

AND OTHER FAIRYTALES
BYRD NASH

Rook and Castle Press

Publisher's Cataloging-in-Publication Data
provided by Five Rainbows Cataloging Services

Names: Nash, Byrd, author.
Title: The wicked wolves of Windsor : and other fairytales / Byrd Nash.
Description: Tulsa, OK : Rook and Castle Press, 2019.
Identifiers: ISBN 978-1-733-45662-3 (paperback) | ISBN 978-0-578-51475-8 (ebook)
Subjects: LCSH: Fairy tales. | Women--Fiction. | Three bears (Tale) | Little Red Riding Hood (Tale) | Fantasy fiction. | Short stories. | BISAC: FICTION / Fantasy / Collections & Anthologies. | FICTION / Fairy Tales, Folk Tales, Legends & Mythology. | FICTION / Short Stories (single author) | FICTION / Women. | GSAFD: Fantasy fiction. | Fairy tales.
Classification: LCC PS3614.A724 W65 2019 (print) | LCC PS3614.A724 (ebook) | DDC 813/.6--dc23.

The lyf so short, the craft so long to learne
Geoffrey Chaucer

Dedications

To the Only One
Fluctuat nec mergitur

The Stories

Milking Time

Bess was milking her favorite cow as her stepmother entered the barn and asked her to kill a sorcerer.

She continued the squeezing rhythm, enjoying the satisfying sound of the liquid stream hitting the tin of the pail. The barn was filled with the low murmur of contented farm animals. The early morning was usually the time of the day she liked best, mostly because she could be private before her family awoke.

"Did you hear me?" her stepmother demanded. Being a short woman, the cow blocked her from seeing the girl's exasperated countenance.

Bess stood up, putting aside pail and stool. She returned the cow to its pen, letting the calf finish off whatever milk was left. She hooked the gate latch, retrieved the milk bucket, and headed back toward the house.

Her stepmother broke into a trot to keep up with the girl's stride, their long dresses whipping behind them.

"Why can't Annie do it?" she finally replied.

"You know how she is about blood!" protested her stepmother. "Remember what happened at the last fall butchering?"

Her ever-practical stepmother did have a point, admitted Bess. Her half-sister Annie had never really taken to farm life and its realities of growing, harvesting, and dying.

She pondered the request while she fitted the top of the stoneware jar with a straining cloth. While Bess poured the milk her stepmother tapped her foot impatiently.

"What's he done that requires killing?"

"He's been winning at cards, dice, you name it. Taking the hard earned pay from the farmers as thoughtlessly as a child plucks a summer daisy."

Bess felt no sympathy. She hadn't forgotten how, after Father's death, their neighbors had gossiped the land would now sell cheaply. But we didn't sell, the girl thought with grim satisfaction.

Bess looked down on hands that were no longer soft and white but were calloused and red-chapped and replied in a mild tone, "Maybe they should be going home instead of swilling ale at The Pipers?"

"Annie's young man, Trevor, is one of those farmers. He could lose the wedding dowry his father gave him," her stepmother said, adding mournfully, "if he hasn't already."

In the gloom of the root cellar, Bess said nothing aloud about this potential for catastrophe. Neither of them cared for the match between Annie and Trevor. Probably because he was the type who would wager his bridal savings with a stranger at a local posting inn.

"I'll go in this evening and see for myself."

Her stepmother smiled, patting Bess' arm. "I knew you'd take care of it."

When his city business had failed, her father brought his family to the country. From the windows of their hired coach, all Bess saw was a dark, small cottage and a falling-down barn.

Seeking reassurance, the young girl had turned helplessly to her stepmother. There she found only blank horror on the woman's face.

It took three years before Father's dream of a pastoral paradise finally wore out his heart with life's reality. Sent to the fields to bring him lunch, Bess had discovered his corpse in the dirt behind the plow, the patient farm horse standing still in his traces.

Country life had already taught Bess that work couldn't be left unfinished. Carefully stepping over her father's body, she completed the furrow. Afterward, she brought him home across the back of the horse where he was greeted by the wails of his wife and youngest daughter.

In the face of this calamity, her stepmother proved smarter than her husband by immediately admitting she knew nothing about farming. Instead of trying to manage the land she turned the farm over to Bess, who had already shown aptitude and interest.

For herself, she said, "Ladies will be tired of dullness," predicting that a market for fine goods would soon flourish since the war with Napoleon had ended.

Her stepmother's prophecy came true as the fancywork she had taken to town was appreciated and admired. It seemed city ladies were ready to spend their coin on beautiful things to decorate themselves and their homes.

With a growing demand for her work, her stepmother taught her needlework skills to her daughter Annie who proved an eager pupil.

Recently turned sixteen, Annie much preferred the genteel picture of sitting at a window in a fresh, clean dress, plying a needle rather than feeding chickens and milking cows.

Amusements were thin and so just a few months before, settled about a winter's fire, Annie had proposed a wager. To Bess, she suggested they see who would be first to draw a husband to their door.

They paid no heed to their mother's statement that "To marry in haste was to repent at leisure." Willing to do anything to alleviate the tedium, Bess agreed and the girls shook on the deal.

With whispered secrets and giggles the cold weeks flew faster now. Poppets were quickly hidden under their pillows if Mother ventured by their shared room.

When Trevor arrived at the farm, looking for a lost hunting dog, the three women exchanged knowing looks behind his back.

They welcomed the tired traveler to their table for a bite of supper. He was served off their fine city dishes, one of the few things saved from their creditors, and given the choicest piece of meat.

Annie shot Bess a triumphant look across the table.

What passed for a village lay a distance of five miles from the farm which gave Bess plenty of time to think about her sister's suitor.

"Trevor," muttered Bess darkly to herself. Her stride grew faster in response to her inner agitation.

No other man had arrived to court so Annie's

Cunning Work was declared the winner. Still, Bess did not envy her half-sister her choice for not only was Trevor a poor catch being a second son but Bess thought him without integrity.

Her dismal thinking almost caused the girl to miss the turn toward the village at the crossroads. Catching herself in time, Bess stopped and looked about to make sure no one was in view.

To work the Glamour that her stepmother insisted she wear, Bess spat on her finger and drew a quick sigil on the center of her forehead, the wrists of her arms, and the toes of her boots.

Turning clockwise she pulled down the Glamour over her face and form, changing her appearance.

Settled into her new skin, Bess braced her shoulders and took a step forward: time to take the measure of this spell-caster's mettle.

The Piper was an old building of thick timber and stone, in a Tudor style. Its size often made the villagers brag that it must have been an old manor house, perhaps once owned by Squire Ackerman's family.

In her former town life, Bess had once seen the Squire's mighty fine house and estate. She doubted that a man with real glass windows would have called the Piper home.

Regardless of its past glory, today it served the

needs of travelers and tradesmen going through to the large city beyond. But what the inn really did best was ladle out gossip to its patrons.

As Bess approached the building a group of laborers stood on the stoop, blocking the doorway. Their refusal to give way forced the girl to squeeze through them to gain entrance.

It was an intimidation game that Bess usually avoided by going around to the back door. Today, feeling irritated by their boorish behavior, she used her powers to give one a discreet electric shock. Bess hid a smile as he cursed, spilling his tankard.

The Piper's current owners were Stoney and Maggie Tolliver. Town-bred like Bess and her family, they had owned the inn only for a few years and so were still viewed suspiciously as newcomers.

Stoney was at the counter, working the bar. He was a former sailor, a small, dark-haired, wiry man who moved with quick grace as he served the crowd their drinks.

"You want Megs?" he asked her and tossed his head back, nodding behind him. "She'll be in the kitchen."

The outdoor kitchen was behind the inn in a former courtyard enclosure with four stone walls higher than Bess' head. During the summer months, extra tables and benches would be set up for weddings and funerals as the area was quite large.

A set of buildings along the perimeter that had once been stables now housed chickens, ducks, and a sow named Grandella.

Bess found Maggie pulling fresh bread loaves out of a dome-shaped oven using a long paddle board. Each loaf was placed into a basket and the smell of the fine bread made the girl's mouth water.

Maggie was dark like her husband and her face was flushed from the heat of the oven. In her exertion, strands of black hair had escaped from under her cap and now blew in front of her eyes.

"Oh!" Megs cried out in surprise when she finally noticed Bess. She laughed self-consciously before adding, "You're the answer to a prayer! There's too many dining tonight for Stoney and me to handle. Can you help us out?"

Bess had not lived three years in abject poverty to not know the value of her labor.

She had already noticed the Piper's famous sow was suckling a new batch of family members. Grandella produced exceptional offspring of the highest quality and the many trophies displayed in the inn's great room stood as proof that Stoney's bragging had merit.

"I can help in exchange for a piglet from Grand's litter."

"Now that's a bit much for one night's work…" began Megs, narrowing her eyes. She also knew the value of Grandella's farrow.

"I'll give you five days of work, including sweeping, mopping, laundry and making beds," Bess emphasized each task by unfolding a finger on her hand.

"And I'll settle for the runt. She'll kill it anyway."

"Well, you'll have to agree on the number of work days with Stoney, but I am that desperate for the help," conceded Maggie. "Men! Men don't realize everything that needs doing!"

Ready to earn herself a piglet, Bess grabbed up the baskets to take back inside. Working side by side with Maggie made Bess realize the truth of her friend's comment.

Stoney stayed at the bar throughout the evening, talking and spinning tales, picking up coins to put in the metal box kept under the counter. Meanwhile, the two women cooked the dinners, cut bread and cheese, carried serving trays, and collected the dirty dishes.

The cycle of serving, collecting, and washing never seemed to end. However, her work let Bess ask questions without being obvious about her real interest.

"Why so busy tonight?"

"It's been getting busier every night since *that man* came ten days ago," grumbled Maggie. She quickly added, forcing a more cheerful tone to her words, that rang rather falsely, "but that's been good for business."

"I heard something about that…?"

"I'm sure your mother has heard about *him*,"

confided Megs, always ready for a gossip. "That no-good Trevor has been in every night this week. He's been mewing after *that man* like a toddler refusing to be weaned."

Bess never thought it a good policy to criticize family or soon-to-be-family to others, so she just shrugged.

"Annie and he haven't posted the banns yet, so the coin is his own."

Maggie clucked like one of her hens as she used tongs to pull drumsticks out from the cast iron pan.

"He's not the only one here spending his coin as if he was the county squire, so perhaps I'm being too harsh. They do love to be entertained by our guest."

"Oh, so the man is an entertainer?"

Maggie gave a snort, coupled with raised eyebrows.

"He's an entertainment of some sort. You'll see."

Bess was stacking dishes from the tables onto a tray so her back was to the staircase when the general chatter of the room suddenly quieted.

Bess moved to stand in the front hall alcove, so she was half sheltered by wall and drapery. From her position, she could view the stranger unobserved.

The newcomer was enormously fat, a huge man that topped her own beanpole height by at least two hands. His labored breathing was raspy and the oak stair risers groaned under his weight as he came down them.

He was dressed in the height of finery with tailored clothes and on each of his fat fingers was a ring of gold holding a colored stone. From his vest chain dangled a crystal fob the size of a pigeon's egg.

By the time he was four steps short of the landing the dining room had become oppressively silent as if royalty or a two-headed goat had come among them.

He looked expensive and rich. He had presence.

He reeked of sorcery.

Bess bit her own thumbnail as she watched the power of the man's Glamour rise like steam from a pile of cow dung on a cold day. The foggy wisps moved away from him, to hover over the heads of those who he passed.

The stranger greeted many by name as he moved among them, clasping hands and tapping shoulders. His jovial remarks invited them into an intimate circle of friendship while they unknowingly inhaled the invisible smoke of his magic.

One man jumped up from his seat, to wave the sorcerer over to his bench, telling him he had saved a spot for him. Bess pursed her lips in aggravation as she recognized the fool as Trevor.

Dumb as that cockerel who refused to stop crowing last summer. The only way to shut that rooster up had been to kill him.

In disgust, she cleaned her hands on the towel

hanging at her waist before she lifted up the heavy tray to head back to the kitchen.

She had seen enough.

Mother was right.

The sorcerer needs to go.

"Best do it now," advised Maggie, with her arms plunged up to their elbows in hot, soapy water as she washed plates.

"Now?" repeated Bess, puzzled.

As part of their agreement, one of Bess' tasks was to clean the bedrooms of the guests staying at the Piper. However, with so many dishes still to do, surely Maggie could use her help in the kitchen.

"He never leaves his room unless it's to gamble with *them*," explained the innkeeper. "He's already been down at least an hour, so nip upstairs and do what needs doing."

Sensing the girl's reluctance, Maggie added, "That is if you want that piglet. The runt's a girl this time."

The room smelled of the heavy musk of male magic. Despite the evening chill, Bess opened the bottle-glass window and breathed in the fresh air.

The lodger's room was at the back of building and thus gave a good view of the courtyard. It gave Bess ideas, but for now she had work to get done.

With the terrible efficiency that often gave her mother equal parts awe and horror, Bess soon had the room cleared away to her satisfaction. While stripping the bed she discovered some coarse black hairs. These she carefully wrapped inside the clean handkerchief that her mother insisted both the girls carry.

Snapping off a piece of twig from her broom, she dipped it into the chamber pot and then carefully wrapped a napkin around it. Both small bundles Bess dropped out of the window, to the courtyard below, where she would collect them later.

Her last deed was to grasp the handle of the Ash broom and sweep it in concentric circles, Widdershins, across the bare floor.

The girl hummed and sang until every corner of the room had met the ends of her Birch twigs and broomcorn. She swept the pile of dirt out the doorway and said, "Good riddance to you."

Due to his heavy, shuffling tread, Bess had time to get into position. As he threw open the door the view that greeted him was of her counting a pile of coins she had spilled from his purse onto the bed.

He might be fat but he was fast and powerful. In a few steps he reached her and twisted her arm behind her back. Bess cried aloud in pain.

"What are you doing?" the man hissed angrily, spraying her ear with spit, as he searched her pockets.

She uttered a few silly denials which earned her more pain before confessing, "She told me to do it."

"The innkeeper? That bitch..." began the sorcerer

but Bess was quick to contradict him lest Maggie and Stoney find themselves in trouble.

"No, no! *She* told me, she *told* me…"

The sorcerer released her but slapped her with casual brutality across the cheek. The blow sent her reeling backwards to land again on the bed. Bess felt as if she had been downed by a bear. He leaned over her prone position, threatening her with an upraised fist.

"Who? Who told you? Are you the village idiot?"

Up close his eyes were small amongst folds of cheek fat. His face was such an unhealthy color of purple that Bess rather hoped a heart attack would save her some trouble.

"The sorceress," the girl gasped behind a hand she held up to conceal her mouth and blistered cheek. Her words stopped the next blow in mid-strike. Bess dropped her eyes to hide their triumph.

"I *knew* there was someone here. It's the only reason I've stayed in this hell-hole backwater this long," he said. Jubilant, he rubbed his hands together while his fat pink tongue traced around a wet mouth in excitement.

"They told me… warned me not to test her… but I'm hungry, starving for another taste of power."

Noticing the skinny serving girl scuttling away on all fours to the door, he kicked her backside. His boot sent her sprawling face down on the oak floorboards.

"I'm hungry, did you hear?" He said louder, poking her ribs with his shoe to emphasize each word. "Where is she? I can't wait to eat... meet her. Tell me and I'll let you go with just a beating, wench."

"She'll kill me!" cried Bess, cowering and holding her arms over her head.

"You'll have nothing to worry about once I'm done with the witch," said the sorcerer. "However, I could make your life very difficult."

He made a coarse gesture, thrusting his hips forward. Bess swallowed bile.

"She'll be here tonight. That's all I can say, as my life is worth it."

"Tonight?" He sat down on the bed, the mattress sagging to touch the floor. His weight strained the ability of the rope sling in the bed frame to support him.

"Why tonight? Why *here?*"

"It's a full moon. She does magic on the pig every month at the full moon. Grandella is no ordinary pig. Ask anyone."

"A magic pig?" He looked at her with a frown before laughing, remembering the praise he had heard in the tavern for the sow.

"I've heard something about this pig from these country yokels. I put it down to the inbred boasts of the insular ignorant." Ignoring her, he laid down on the bed, patting his large girth.

"Tonight I will do something I've never done before: conquer a pig-witch."

He chortled and told her to go as he was tired. Bess hastily complied.

After closing the door, Bess ran down the stairs only to collide with Trevor who stopped her rapid descent by grabbing her wrist. He dragged her into a small antechamber where the gentry had private teas while waiting for their carriages to be ready.

"What are you up to?" he demanded. "You're always watching me with those judging eyes. I don't trust you."

He held the arm the sorcerer had misused and she barely restraining herself from punching Trevor in the face. However, Bess knew hurting her sister's swain would put Annie in a position of defending her lover. This would only entrench her sister on a path that Bess and her mother considered disastrous.

"I'm helping Stoney and Megs. For one of Grand's piglets."

"He'd never barter one of Grand's piglets," he replied, shaking her by the arm again.

"It's the runt," Bess explained while grimacing at the pain. "Grand will kill it anyway."

He had heard her say many times that she wanted one of Grand's offspring so Trevor let her go. As he stepped away to leave, Bess couldn't resist one parting question.

"Have you lost *all* of the settlement your father gave you?"

"That's none of your business, Bess!"

So the money was gone, or near enough, thought Bess.

Once the full moon cleared the top of the Piper's roof, its glow illuminated the old courtyard and the drama about to unfold.

The sorcerer was standing in the middle of the inn's courtyard. He still wore his earlier finery as his black eyes searched the shadows for his adversary.

"I feel you, witch. Come out and face your fate."

"My fate?" questioned a beautiful and womanly voice, "so you put yourself on the level of gods to decide such?"

The sorceress stepped from the shadows, garbed in a long white dress with draping that recalled ancient times and temple acolytes. She was tall and stately, her long profile, wide brow, and slim neck of the type that rode to war with their breasts bare and their hands clasping a drawn sword.

"I was told you wished to make my acquaintance."

"Nay, not a meeting but a battle," he said, odd shadows distorted the cast of his features making him more monster than man in appearance. They were the same in height but from eating magic he was triple the size of the woman's slim form.

"I heard rumors that someone of power resided in this sewage ditch of a village."

She gave a smile of pleasant disdain as if she had received a compliment by a suitor far beneath her notice. The sorcerer continued his oratory with a sneer.

"You won't be the first I've swallowed, my little country bumpkin."

"Do you think you are *my* first?" she countered, her tone coy. "My dear sir, I hope you are not laboring under some misconception. I'm no trembling virgin, waiting with bated breath for her first kiss of a challenge."

She gave a pretty little yawn, covering her sculptured, full lips with long, tapered fingers before continuing.

"I do have cows that need milking soon. Shockingly early hours in the country you know. So let's get this tiresome meeting done. If I recall the protocol of such matters, you are the challenger, thus I chose the form."

He gave a courtly bow, slow and measured, his left hand going towards her as if inviting her to be his partner in a dance.

"I chose the forms: each must be found in a barnyard."

At her words, in a blink, they both changed: he into the form of a draft horse, a black stallion of great height. His massive and powerful hindquarters propelled his bulk towards her in a rush.

Yet, where she had stood was now also a horse, a fine-boned chestnut mare of madness and savagery, her hooves sharp as knives. Instead of clashing chest to chest, she dodged aside. Her hooves raked a slice across his shoulder, opening flesh as easily as a blade skins a rabbit.

The sorcerer did not pause at the first blooding but spun quickly, slamming his body down across the top of her back. His neck snaked forward, teeth snapping but his attempt to grab her neck met nothing.

She had transformed to a small donkey and nimbly ducked under his wide girth. His miss caused him to land with a hard jolt, stumbling.

The jenny gave a double barrel kick aimed at his ribs but this time it was her own blow that missed connection. The sorcerer was no longer horse but mastiff. His dog muzzle grabbed a donkey leg in mid-kick.

His lips pulled back in a grin as he began to crunch down to break bone. But in relishing his premature triumph the sorcerer had waited too long. She vanished - becoming a tiny flea on the top of his nose.

Grandella lifted her head to watch the commotion as the mastiff ran in circles, angrily shaking his head, and howling. Despite the clamor, the Piper's windows remained dark and shuttered.

"Come out, come out!" he howled.

The girl's flirtatious voice replied, "I dare not, kind sir."

Enraged, the sorcerer went through a rapid-fire sequence of forms: tomcat, rat, gander, and rooster. Finally noticing Grandella, he became a boar and his thick hide proved impervious to the flea's bites.

With his last change, the sorceress quickly exchanged her own form. From flea to chicken, riding his back, the hen's beak plucked out one of the boar's coarse body hairs.

In triumph, she jumped off the boar and the sorceress returned to her natural form. She held the hair in one hand and a small, crude wax carving of a pig in the other.

"Thank you for providing the last element I needed to make your transformation permanent."

The sorceress spat on the carving and pressed the single hair into the malleable tallow wax. As her spell froze his form permanently into a hog, the enraged sorcerer spun about the courtyard in a frenzy, giving desperate, pleading squeals.

Bess watched him with pleased satisfaction.

"I think I shall call you Herbie."

Mother eventually got used to the pig like all the other animals Bess had brought home over the years.

However, the heavy coin purse that accompanied him made the new acquisition even more welcome.

"I thought about returning a portion back to Trevor," began the tall blond woman with the face of a goddess and still wearing the sheets she had borrowed from the Piper's beds.

"However, I figured he'd spend it on some other worthless endeavor. Besides, without his stake, I don't think Annie will find him quite as appealing. Do you, Mother?"

"We'll just keep this back for our own rainy day," her parent reassured her. Tucking the purse into her skirt pocket, the women closed the gate on their new hog pen.

As the seasons turned again, the village grew sleepy with winter. A few coins from the rainy day fund made life in the cottage much easier and the roof was repaired and meat was at the table twice a week.

Mother made plans on opening an exclusive shop in the city. Annie, promised the role as mother's assistant, was too busy to visit with Trevor. As the weeks passed into spring, the intensity of the courtship started to wane.

But for Bess it had always been about the farm.

Herbie had proved himself a productive sire. Bartering his breeding services had given them money enough to hire a girl for managing the garden. It was already looking better with nice tidy rows of spring lettuce.

Bess strolled across the yard in the early morning, a milk pail in hand, feeling good about the farm's prospects. Whistling, she placed her stool under her favorite milking cow, the very first sorceress who had challenged her. She gave the cow a loving pat as her mother entered the barn.

Seeing her parent, Bess put both hands on her hips and demanded, "Not another sorcerer?"

"No!" Her parent's voice held happy excitement so the girl relaxed, sitting down on her stool, reaching for the cow's teats.

"It's Squire Ackerman from Braydock," said her mother. "He heard about our pig and wants to buy him!"

"He's not for sale," Bess replied automatically.

She neither sold nor butchered any of the livestock she had acquired through her magical duels. The girl mentally corrected herself: except for that one rooster that would not stop crowing. For their sanity his death was necessary but they hadn't eaten him. She had buried him in the woods under a good Hawthorn.

Her mother noticed Bess was wearing her true form.

"Daughter, did you forget to change this morning? Do it now and go talk to him. Think what a man of his stature could pay for that pig's breeding services."

When Bess still had not replied, her mother

begged. "Think of the rainy day fund!"

Finally, Bess agreed to talk with the squire. Watching her mother's back as she walked away, the girl muttered to herself, "But I'm not changing."

Squire could take her or leave her.

Besides, she had begun to suspect her mother of being disingenuous about the reason why she insisted on her step-daughter hiding her true beauty. Was it to make Bess appear dull and stupid so the limited number of available men would see only Annie?

She continued to grumble about how the rich made life inconvenient for the poor as she stomped off at a rapid pace, looking down at the ground. When she rounded the corner she crashed into the Squire and would have fallen except he caught her.

She looked up into the blue eyes of the man her Cunning had called to her doorstep. He smiled and said, "Beg pardon."

Bess smiled back.

She would never have to milk a cow again.

Unless she wanted to.

The Wicked Wolves
of Windsor

I'm not going to eat you," said the wolf as he kept pace with the bicycle. "I only want to talk."

Doireann peddled faster and kept her eyes resolutely ahead. She had passed the Great Oak and was going through the heart of Windsor Forest, the estate that surrounded the castle. The dirt track was the only route from Granny Horn's home to the village.

She pretended not to see the beast's red eyes and the tongue as large as her hand, gaping from a mouth full of jagged teeth. He was not a natural beast. Wolves were certainly not a common occurrence in England this late summer of 1918.

"Stay on the path and you'll be safe," Granny Horn had told her when she complained. "That's the rule."

The advice galled Doireann; at fifteen she found it easy to be annoyed by old people.

If she wanted to keep her weekday job helping the postmistress this was the only way she could go. Biting her lip, the red-headed girl kept her hands death-locked on the handlebars, keeping the tires steady as it rode over the ruts.

"Do what you have to do," said Doireann to herself, repeating one of her mother's favorite phrases.

The wolves had started following her in the spring. The beasts always appeared after she passed the Great Oak, ravaged by lightning but still holding a few black branches to the sky.

Mostly it was two or three of the dirty beasts and once as many as five. Sometimes it would be one, like today.

Last summer, one of the wolves had jumped suddenly in front of her tires. Surprised, she hit the brake too hard and almost swerved off the path. As she righted her bicycle, her freckled face red hot with embarrassment and anger, she was greeted by howls of wolfish laughter.

Yes, she had plenty of experience with their dirty tricks.

Today's companion had a small notch in his right ear and a white mane around his neck. This one's tongue had always been honeyed, unlike the others who would make nasty comments about the color of her hair or called her Irish mother a witch.

Still, Doireann didn't trust him.

If anything, she suspected he was the worst of the lot.

The girl stood up from the saddle to pump the pedals harder, making the machine sway from side to side. She wished it would transport her over the miles in an instant so she wouldn't have to listen to his nonsense.

"Doesn't Herne have some duties for you, you nasty creature," she said under her panting breath.

"He will in three days, my dear child," replied the wolf, who had very keen hearing. He saw it as progress that Doireann Horn at long last directly addressed him.

"When that night comes and the full moon travels the sky, we shall be very busy. Why don't you ride the Hunt with us? A witch's get would be welcomed by our master."

Doireann ignored this sally regarding her dead mother. Being Irish, she had heard this and worse. Some ignorant fools even whispered Cathleen Kennedy had caught William Horn with an enchantment.

If anyone had cast a spell it must have been her father. When her Irish mother left her homeland to marry, Cathleen Kennedy had lost family and position as the daughter of a prosperous shopkeeper. In marrying Doireann's father, one gamekeeper among many employed by the large Windsor estate, she had stepped down the social ladder.

Fallen off it, more likely, Doireann thought darkly.

Mother was dead, just one of many who succumbed to the Great Influenza pandemic that had swept across the world. The Great War took Father on the field of Flanders.

Orphaned, Doireann was forced to quit school to help her grandmother. They lived in a ramshackle hovel that the Windsor estate manager had leased to them at a nominal fee out of pity.

Pity, hah! Not much better than a lean-to! The roof leaked and we have to chop firewood to cook our meals.

Doireann forgot the wolf, lost in other, more pressing, resentments. Considering the unfairness of her situation kept her mind so busy she was surprised to discover the wolf had vanished. But they always did when she had passed the boundary marker, leaving the dark forest well behind her.

She sighed and slowed her pedaling until the machine stopped. Straddling the bicycle to keep it from falling, she straightened her straw hat and tucked stray hairs behind her ears.

Best to enter the village with some semblance of decency and decorum.

Doireann had passed the vicarage, grocer, and school when she came upon a few of the local boys up to mischief. They were throwing rocks at a black cat that had taken refuge under a rosebush.

The young girl couldn't stand bullies.

Outraged, Doireann braked and threw the bicycle hard to the ground. She jumped off before it landed, holding her long skirt aside so it wouldn't catch in the machine's chain.

"Stop that, you ruffians!" When they paid no heed to her command, she scooped a handful of rocks from the path and pelted them at the boys' backs.

"I see you, Tom Roberts! I'll be sure to tell Constable Brown what you get up to when you should be in school."

Whether it was her accurate shots or the threat of the local law, the three boys sprang away, running down the street. Satisfied, she turned to collect her bicycle but was stopped by a purring voice.

"Thank you, dear child."

The black cat, belly still low to the ground, looked side to side as she crept out from the low-hanging roses. The creature was small, her eyes green as apples, and her toes neat and tiny.

"Your mother sends a message. Take the key and use it the first night."

Before Doireann could recover from her astonishment, the cat shot away, racing across the park lawn. With tail held high, it disappeared from sight.

Doireann turned back to where the cat had been to see a gold gleam. Under the rosebush was a large key.

Crouching down, she reached under the leaves and picked it up. It was heavy and old. Pocketing it, the girl collected her bicycle, and walked the rest of the way to the post office, deep in thought.

Doireann's work at the post office wasn't strenuous or even very difficult. Her duties were to dust shelves, sweep floors, and mind the counter when Post Mistress O'Donnell couldn't.

Sometimes she was allowed to wrap packages to the standard that the mail service required.

Doireann sometimes thought the only reason she held the position was Mrs. O'Donnell was lonely for company. She was Catholic and Irish, like Doireann, in a town filled with Church of England.

It was surprising she was able to hold the position at all considering.

Mrs. O'Donnell had managed the post office for months during her husband's illness. By the time he died, the residents had grown accustomed to her taking his place.

Upon his death, she had formally applied for her

husband's position. At first, the government was reluctant to appoint a mere woman to such an important job. However, when some clever chap suggested that being a woman her salary could be halved, Mrs. O'Donnell was officially endorsed.

In her position as post mistress, Mrs. O'Donnell knew much of the gossip. Perhaps she could give Doireann a better idea on how to deal with her problem.

"I was talking with someone yesterday about that local legend - the Wolves of Windsor. Do you remember it, Mrs. O'Donnell?"

"Thank goodness, they've finally approved that Treaty of Versailles. About time I warrant."

Mrs. O'Donnell clucked over her newspaper. "I've been reading here about what our boys endured during the Great War. Filthy conditions. No wonder so many of them didn't come back. Terrible."

Finally, she looked up over her reading glasses at her young helper who was sweeping the floor.

"The Wolves of Windsor? That's just an old story. I'm surprised someone as young as you would know it. Just a folktale for when the wind howls outside the door and the rain lashes the window casements so hard you think they'll break."

"But what *is* the tale? *Exactly?*"

"Depends on who tells the story. Some say it's Herne the Hunter running with the fairies to steal stray livestock. However, that is nasty pagan thinking."

Mrs. O'Donnell paused in her story to cross herself before continuing with her own pet theory.

"Personally, I believe it's Satan collecting his sinners. They won't know any peace until Gabriel sounds his horn. Makes far more sense to my way of thinking."

Before Doireann could ask any more questions their discussion was interrupted by the door opening. It was Mrs. Babcock with a request for postage.

"How are you, Dory Anne?"

As the girl bristled at the mispronunciation of her name, the post-mistress inserted diplomatically, "Dirren is about to go check my hens for the day. By the way, how are yours laying, Mrs. Babcock?"

She was glad to escape Mrs. Babcock. Besides, feeding the chickens Mrs. O'Donnell kept in her tiny allotment behind the post office was one of her favorite unofficial chores.

Doireann loved to collect the hen's eggs, rubbing her fingers across their shells of sky blue and freckled brown. Whenever she pulled one from its hiding spot, she felt she had discovered treasure.

She latched the door on the coop and turned to go back indoors when her eye was caught by the rapid, busy motion of a group of wrens. They flitted in and about the dense brush of Mrs. O'Donnell's neglected garden.

The wren's heads were dull russet, making

Doireann smile and murmur, "Like me."

Reaching into her pocket, the girl pulled out her lunch sandwich. She would gladly sacrifice some for the wrens as the bread was quite stale.

She also sprinkled out what was left in the hen's feed bucket before she took a seat on the back step. Doireann tucked her knees up and wrapped her arms around them as she watched the little brown bobs come to peck at her gift.

The girl sat very still as one came closer. The creamy mark along the wren's black eye gave the bird an intelligent, quizzical look as she gazed up at the girl.

"Dear child, thank you. Your mother sends a message. Take the comb and use it the second night."

Startled, Doireann jerked back causing the bird to wing away to the safety of the tree. Looking down, she found a solid gold comb at the toe of her shoe.

She picked it up and ran her fingers over the teeth. Thoughtfully, she put it into her skirt's pocket to join the key.

On the way home, Doireann took time to stop at the cemetery where her mother had been buried.

While the doctor had ruled the cause of death to be exhaustion from the Influenza pandemic, Doireann also blamed her mother's Irish stubbornness. For Cathleen Kennedy Horn, running a high fever and delirious, had insisted on carrying through with her chores.

Eventually, she was found dead by Doireann and Granny Horn under the clothesline on a gray, rainy day. It was probably the only rest the woman had had since she married.

The gravestone paid for by the Gamekeeper's Trust for Widows was stark and plain. Doireann stared at it for a moment before kneeling by the mound of earth. She started cleaning away the weeds, tossing the dandelions behind the headstone, as she talked.

"What do you mean by these gifts, mother? How am I supposed to know what you want me to do if you don't tell me plain and simple?"

When she finished, Doireann sat on the soft grass next to where her mother's body lay. She shed a few tears as an offering and uttered a short prayer.

"I miss you, Mother."

A rabbit peered around the edge of the headstone with dandelions hanging from her mouth.

"Dear child, thank you. Your mother sends a message. Take the mirror and use it on the third night."

Doireann leapt up at the rabbit's words. She saw her white tail flashing as the rabbit bolted to take refuge in the thick hedge that bordered the church grounds.

The girl looked down to see her mother's last gift: a

mirror, held in a locket of gold, at her feet.

From the post office to Granny's home took an hour to travel even on a bicycle. Granny's cottage was isolated, surrounded by the ancient wood, and it was another thing Doireann hated about living there.

Once Doireann crossed the boundary marker at the edge of the Windsor forest she would pass no more houses or farms.

The wolf running beside her noticed Doireann's distraction and asked about her day. The path was so narrow it placed the wolf right by her side. His black fur coat and white ruff were so near she could have reached out and touched him without leaving the path.

She ignored the temptation and continued to look straight ahead.

"Tell me about the Wolves of Windsor. The real story."

When he didn't reply, she added, "Or does that break your rules?"

"No," he said, "but telling you won't bring you any comfort."

Doireann laughed and said sarcastically, "Being harassed every day without cause by wicked wolves doesn't make my life comfortable."

He gave a playful leap in the air at her comment before galloping to catch up with her.

"You scored a point there, Red. But remember, there are things that, knowing them, could make you feel much worse."

"I'm a little tired of people telling me what I should or shouldn't know." She stood up from the saddle and was about to peddle faster when he started to talk.

"We are all cursed, Red. Cursed men and women. We didn't play by society's rules and we stand punished for it."

"Criminals, murderers, and thieves. Just as I thought."

Her judgmental comment was greeted by a long howl.

"Was I to let my wife and children starve? Was I to let them die of hunger? One king's rabbit got me into a wolf's coat."

"Poacher! Taker of property not your own though I'm sure you did more than that," the girl accused him.

"I promise you no more. Would you believe me if I could cross myself as they do in your church? I was punished for simply snaring the king's rabbit. But my grave error was taking it from the woods where Herne rules."

"Rules are made for a reason," countered Doireann sanctimoniously. She would give no quarter to these creatures.

"Rules didn't keep your mother safe," the wolf snapped back harder, his words more biting than the girl's scorn.

"Cathleen Kennedy broke your rules and loved a man she couldn't marry. At least she got the peace of death. Whereas I'm cursed until I find another to take my place."

Doireann, the loss of her mother fresh in her mind, retorted angrily, "Don't speak of my mother! You didn't know her at all!"

"I didn't? Who do you think she told her troubles to when she went into town?" countered the wolf. He cocked his head, his ears forward. "She wouldn't be pleased to hear you quit school."

"You think I *wanted* to quit school? I did what I had to do to help Granny," she muttered between clenched teeth.

Angry tears blurred Doireann's vision. She felt her pale face flush with heat, in a way only redheads could burn.

"She was worried for you, Red. Wanted something better for her only daughter."

"Shut up!" Doireann stopped her bicycle as she couldn't see the path any more because of the tears.

She dug into her pockets and grabbed the rocks she had collected in town; the boys attacking the cat had given her ideas. Pulling them out, she pelted them at the wolf but was blind to if they made contact.

"A friendly warning, Red," he howled back at her as he left, "A gift for the friendship I had with your mother. When is the moon is full, stay home. If you can."

When she finally made it to Granny's she discovered her father had not died in Flanders. Instead, he was sitting at her grandmother's table, eating the last of the roast chicken.

Her grandmother happily babbled, explaining how the war office had made a mistake. Her son, Doireann's father, had been found in a small hospital in France, suffering from shell shock.

"Your dear dad is home from the War. Aren't you going to say anything?" demanded her father, grinning.

"Indeed, how lucky we are," his daughter finally replied, her voice numb.

Once Doireann had wondered why her gentle mother had ever married such a man, but after her burial, she had discovered her birth certificate. Noting the date, she knew a woman pregnant with no ring, had few choices.

His face was meaner and uglier than Doireann remembered. Mistaking the reason for her stare, William Horn tapped the new scar that ran from his right eyebrow and into his hairline.

"A Kraut shell. Didn't kill me but wiped out my

platoon." Her father wiped his greasy mouth as he gestured her closer. "Come now Cathleen and do your duty. Give me a kiss of welcome."

"She looks like her mother more each day," said Granny Horn, hearing her son speak his wife's name.

Doireann reluctantly dragged herself over to her father where he roughly grabbed her, forcing her to sit on his knee. He kissed her cheek before moving his mouth over hers, forcing it open under a slobbering assault.

Her struggles made William Horn laugh before he shoved her away.

"Mother, I need more." He pounded his fist on the table with such force that the plates rattled. Granny ran about the kitchen to serve him.

Doireann watched her father shove more food into his mouth as older childhood memories surfaced: of violence, his attacks on her mother, the leers and gropes.

She wanted to vomit as she understood her mother's gift of a key.

The cottage had two bedrooms. One had been her parents' and, after her mother's death, Granny had taken it. But now the old woman happily returned it to its former owner and shared Doireann's narrow bed.

Once Granny Horn started snoring, a scratching noise began at the door.

"Doireann, Doireann, open up."

She ignored his voice and closed her eyes tight. The door had no mechanical lock but she had placed the key at the threshold.

She prayed it would be enough.

"Cathleen, Cathleen, open up."

The door rattled but it did not open.

The next day was Saturday so Doireann did not go to work. Instead, she tried to do her chores around the cottage.

Her father decided that the War had given him privilege. He sat in a chair on the front porch, smoking his pipe, watching her, always watching her, as she moved around the yard.

His eyes stalked her like a dog watched sheep.

It was worse when he would creep up behind her, surprising her with a grab around her waist, his powerful arms painfully squeezing her breasts.

"Cathleen give me a kiss!" he would beg.

Doireann would be forced to pay a toll with a peck on the cheek or he wouldn't release her. He laughed hoarsely and spanked her on the bottom as she ran back to the house.

When she had asked her grandmother for help the old woman had pretended not to understand. Perhaps she didn't know or couldn't imagine what her son wanted with her granddaughter.

Besides, even if she did know and care, what could Granny do?

The second night, Doireann returned the key to the door's threshold. At the windowsill she arranged the comb, leaning it against the glass, with the tines pointing up.

The girl said her prayers before she climbed into bed. Her heart hammered as she pulled the covers up tightly to her chin.

"Doireann, Doireann, let me in."

The door rattled but when it did not open, she heard his heavy footsteps retreat. He slammed the front door and moments later she heard the tapping on her window glass.

"Cathleen, Cathleen, let me in. Let me in."

But the tines of the comb stretched and became bars. The window did not open though he rapped all night.

"I want more than porridge, Mother."

He was in a foul mood, throwing things about the one small room that served as their kitchen, dining, and living. It had always been too small but now with him occupying it, Doireann felt she and her grandmother were mice sharing a box with a tomcat.

Granny Horn fluttered, wringing her hands, wanting to please but not knowing how. They had only a sack of meal left since William had eaten all else in the cottage.

"We didn't know you were coming home or I'd have gotten something better for you," apologized the old woman. "I'll send Doireann into town on Monday to the grocer."

Doireann didn't know where the money was to come from for new groceries but kept her opinion to herself.

With her head down, she spooned the porridge into her mouth so quickly it burned her tongue. Doireann just wanted to finish and get out of the house but when the girl rose to leave the table, her father stopped her with a vise-like grip around her arm.

"Unlock your door and window tonight, Cathleen. I will have what's due me."

Calling the girl by her mother's name was disturbing enough but the wild madness in his eyes terrified her.

Doireann went to check her bicycle but found both tires flat. She searched the shed for her tire pump but could not find it.

"What are you looking for?" her father shouted from his seat on the porch. The smoke from his pipe masked his features.

"Are you looking for these, girl?"

In his fist he dangled the key and comb.

In a daze, Doireann walked past him, to help Granny with the washing. Behind his back, Doireann's trembling hand touched her neck to confirm the presence of her last gift.

Hanging there, under her blouse lay over her heart the last protection: the mirror in the gold locket.

The girl packed her most precious items: a photo of her mother, the silver baby rattle from relatives she had never met, and some coins she had saved from her salary.

She wore her cycling outfit. Its ankle-length hemline and slim skirt made slipping out the cottage's back window an easy task.

Doireann had only a hazy plan - to get to town and away from her father. The girl took the path trying to be quiet but her boots seemed to make loud noises, snapping twigs and hitting rocks.

Even though the sun had set, the full moon would not crest the treetops for hours. The darkness changed the familiar landmarks and the noises were all strange.

The sudden hoot of an owl drove her into a panicked run which only ended when she tripped over a bootlace that had come untied.

"Stop being a scaredy cat," Doireann told herself, breathing harshly through her nose. She grabbed the boot that had come off in the fall and tugged it back on, savagely knotting the broken laces.

Doireann continued, walking fast, sometimes

trotting but always moving forward. Without her bicycle, the journey in the dark stretched out forever.

"Stay on the path, stay on the path. You'll be safe, you'll be safe," she chanted to herself.

Betting on an old woman's frail grip on sanity was all the girl had and Doireann clasped that hope hard enough to break it.

"Thought you'd run back to that wailing mother of yours, Cathleen?"

Doireann stopped, her shocked heart leaping into her throat as her father emerged from the trees to block her path. He grinned at her alarmed expression.

"A gamekeeper knows his forest, woman."

The girl turned to run but he grabbed her long braid and the yank brought her into his arms. He squeezed her so she couldn't escape, his mouth smearing slimy kisses down her neck as he groped her breasts.

Doireann fought back, kicking as she sobbed and screamed. "I am *not* my mother. I am your *daughter*! I am *your* daughter!"

Her words earned a blow that sent her stumbling to the ground. Hitting the turf, her knapsack fell open and her few treasures were trampled under his boots as he continued his attack.

"Do you need another lesson, Cathleen?" He yanked her back and forth, dragging her over the rough ground, like a rag doll.

William Horn pulled his daughter up and wrapped both of his hands around her neck in a choke-hold. Dangling, her boots off the ground, Doireann saw over his shoulder that the moon had finally crested the top of the trees.

Distantly, she heard the sound of a hunting horn.

"What's this? A gift from another man?"

His violence had popped buttons and ripped open the top of her blouse. Exposed, was her mother's last gift, the gold locket holding the mirror.

One-handed, he snapped the ribbon that held it around her neck, forgetting the girl. He opened the case and the moon glowed down upon its mirrored surface. Whatever he saw made him cradle the locket in both hands, enraptured.

Doireann crawled backwards, like a crab, over the grass. She staggered to her feet but could move no further as they were now surrounded by the Wolves of Windsor.

The legend goes that when the full moon rises and touches the Belt of Orion, Herne the Hunter sounds his horn.

It is time for wise individuals to stay indoors; for valuable livestock to be put away. It is not a night for courting couples to wander, for any off the path Herne can claim as his own.

The wolves chanted as they circled around

Doireann. Her father remained oblivious to the danger; all his attention was for the mirror he held.

"Who to take? Who joins the Hunt?"

The large bodies of the beasts buffeted the girl so roughly she had trouble staying on her feet.

"Two replace two. Two replace two."

"No!" she shouted, "I stayed on the path."

The notched-ear wolf was seated on his haunches at the top of the ditch while his fellows danced below him. He shook his head as if saddened by her behavior.

"You are most clearly off the path, dear child," he said. Doireann broke contact with his gaze to look down at grass; the dirt path lay well behind her.

"Don't say you weren't warned."

"No!" cried Doireann, growing even more angry at the unfairness of it. She stamped her right foot emphatically down on the ground and pointed at the boot with the broken shoelace.

"In my boot, is the earth of the path. And I stand upon it."

At her words, the circling wolves whined in confusion, looking at their leader for guidance. He gave a sharp nod with his muzzle and his fellows fell into a line.

They sat on their haunches, front paws together, facing Doireann and her father like well-trained dogs. The wolves were only waiting for a word from their alpha in order to begin their meal.

Doireann again pronounced herself safe. She forced her words to be firm, like how she talked to Granny when she had one of her spells.

"The path is nothing but dirt. I have it in my shoe. If I am on the path, you cannot take me. Those are the rules. Herne would punish those who take what isn't theirs."

The wolf's red eyes gleamed in merriment at the game she would play. He bowed his head accepting her argument but countered with one of his own.

"If you define the path as such, your father is not on the path's dirt. No gravel. No soil is in his boots. Or his pockets. He is forfeit."

Doireann shot her sire a glance as her thoughts scattered, trying to find a plan that would save them both. He had continued to ignore the peril, not looking up from his mirror. The yapping of the wolves made it difficult for her to think.

"Let her choose! Let her choose!"

She heard the far-off horn sound again; the night was traveling fast and the constellation of Orion was over the treetops.

"Choose one of us now, dear child," commanded their pack leader, "for soon I will no longer be able to hold them."

"I chose you!" She pointed at the white-ruffed wolf. Of all of them, he might have some decency or pity.

The other wolves bowed their heads, accepting her choice. One-by-one, in a line, they departed, casting neither a look to the right nor the left. They melted into the shadows of the wood until only the red-haired girl, her father, and the wolf remained.

"Best go, dear child, and don't look back," the lone wolf recommended.

Doireann scrambled to gather up her belongings: the photo, the rattle, any coins she could see in the moonlight, and started the return walk home.

When the screams behind her started, she ran and ran, but she never looked back.

At breakfast, Granny wondered where her son was.

Her guileless comment caused her granddaughter to choke on her porridge. But, while Doireann felt guilty, she also had the pragmatic realism of the young.

Father could have died honorably in France. He chose differently.

The door opened to admit a man of such size that he blocked the early morning light. His position cast his face in shadow and instinctively, Doireann grabbed the bread knife on the table.

"Fierce little thing you are, Red," commented the newcomer.

He threw a brace of coneys down on Granny Horn's kitchen table. The two women looked at him dumbfounded, while he politely closed the door and took a stool.

"Some of that fine porridge, Mother."

"Son?" queried Doireann's grandmother.

The man was almost the same size as William Horn. But he had dark brown hair, not black; soft brown eyes, instead of ones soaked in madness. But she often got muddled these days so when he said, "Certainly your son," she handed him a bowl.

He dug into the last of their porridge with fervor. Around the instrument in his mouth, he continued talking.

"I've already been up to the castle and got my old job. They insist I start at a junior's pay because of me being gone off to war. If the nobs didn't get us drowned like dogs in the ditches of France, they'll knock us down when we come home."

Granny Horn smacked the back of his head with her dishtowel as she reprimanded him, "Don't be talking like that about our good king and queen."

The fact that the man didn't spring up and smack her back should have told Granny this wasn't her son. Besides who cared about the king and queen of England anyway? Certainly not this Irish girl.

"Put down that knife, Red, before you do yourself an injury."

Doireann watched the man warily, taking note of his notched ear and the thick white scar around his neck. Her grip tightened on the antler handle of the blade.

"I am going back to school," she demanded. "Women can do things now instead of feeding worthless men and doing their laundry."

"Well, that sounds like a good thing to do for a smart girl like you," said the new master of the house. Reaching into the canvas bag that hung off his shoulder, he pulled several objects out, tossing them to her one-by-one.

"You've got plenty of gold to pay for whatever you wish," he indicated the mirror, comb, and key she held.

"Make your own way, Red, or others will make it for you."

Giving her a wolfish grin, he returned to his bowl, licking it clean.

The Queen's Favorite

The queen's favorite was a pretty black mare with large soulful eyes, a dished nose, and a muzzle that could fit into the palm of a child's hand. She arrived with the wedding gifts and was a consummate liar.

Malika's penchant for telling tall tales caused her to be quickly abandoned by all except the queen. She found the horse's stories refreshing due to their brash ridiculousness.

Every day, as the sun rose, the queen would ride her through the secluded park that surrounded the castle. She could be relatively private as the fawning courtiers refused to rise so early and it gave her time to listen to Malika's unrepentant lying.

"Maid Maud was retching out the back door of the kitchen this morning. I believe she is pregnant by Sir Reginald."

"Do you think the baby will be born by midsummer?" Elaine replied, barely suppressing a smile. Sir Reginald was a senior knight in her husband's court, renowned for his Christian piety and courteous treatment of women. The disparity between the pious Sir Reginald and bawdy Maud made a good jest.

Before the mare could respond, the queen's groom rode up beside them. "Best to be getting back, Your Majesty."

He made the request apologetically, but Elaine knew that her morning ritual was at an end for the day. What took precedence were the needs of her husband, King Everard.

"We must return, my lovely one," Elaine lamented as she turned the mare back towards the ramparts. The horse gave a disparaging snort, tossing her head.

"The king can wait."

And that was the biggest lie the horse had ever told.

At age sixteen, Elaine had married King Everard, a man thirty years her senior. Her parents were pleased as the match enriched them with land, coin, and connection. Unwisely, they never questioned why

Everard had searched so far and wide for a bride.

Ten years since her wedding and Queen Elaine still had not borne a child. Her barrenness was not for want of trying; the king took his duties upon her body with tedious regularity.

Only during the three days of the waxing full moon did he ignore her. At that time he retreated into the forest on the pretext of conducting a solitary tramp through his kingdom. He always returned with a satisfied air of contentment and his temperament was improved for a few days afterward so Elaine never questioned his absence.

Besides, those three precious nights gave the queen her only respite.

In whispers behind closed doors, far from the king's chambers, some of the court discussed the situation. They noted while the queen had not become pregnant, neither had any of the king's paramours.

When she returned, the queen headed to the main hall where her husband would hear petitions and court cases from his people. Her attendance was mandatory for as King Everard enjoyed telling others, "What was a king without his queen?"

"About time you arrived," growled Everard. His pallor was that particular hue of green, an indication he was working himself into one of his famous tempers. "Your morning ride kept us waiting."

The queen sat down on the throne, pulling the long heavy train of her gown off to the side. She had learned to keep a placid expression on her face revealing nothing of how she felt. If she said or did anything, it would earn her his ire. On the other hand, if she did not speak when he demanded it also infuriated him.

Today, it was three parties squabbling over land and dowries. It was all a sham - whoever paid the king the most would win his opinion. The king willfully took bribes to fill his coffers and justice was not a thing he ever bedded.

Knowing this, Elaine found it easy to remove her mind to another place, all while appearing to listen. She nodded when required. Once asked by Everard for her opinion, she deferred to his own with an insipid speech about the male superiority in such things.

Last to enter the hall was an old crone garbed in black. With the appearance of the local witch, Elaine shot a surreptitious glance toward her husband. While all in the court professed to be Christian, they would give the witch's words more faith than any sermon by a priest.

The witch announced, "The queen is not happy. That is why she cannot bear."

The hall was silent for the courtiers did not dare even a mutter at the witch's statement. Only one in the court had ever considered the issue of the queen's happiness and he also did not glance toward the dais where the couple sat on their thrones.

King Everard turned to Queen Elaine and with his clenched fist on the arm of his chair asked after her well-being. She responded promptly, "My life is everything that I would wish it to be."

Turning back to the witch, the king asked, contemptuously, "Enlighten us, seer. Tell me what my wife needs to be happy."

"For the horse, Malika, to speak the truth."

The witch had made the king look like a fool and that was something he could not abide. Throughout the day, Queen Elaine felt her husband's rage build: his eyes grew yellow with slits for pupils and his skin took on more of that dangerous green hue.

Elaine wished only to flee so, despite common sense, she slipped away to the stable after supper.

"Why did that witch have to come?" she moaned, watching the mare lip apple slices from her hand. The horse responded, "The king is a pure and gentle knight. He will take the queen's unhappiness as a sign to be a better husband."

"Liar," the queen gently admonished her. But grief made her deaf to danger. She didn't realize she wasn't alone until the king spoke.

"I thought you would be here talking to this

worthless beast," he said, his hand landing on her shoulder as heavy as the fall of a gallow's floor.

Everard's grip crept up to clasp the back of her neck and Elaine froze under it. She knew stillness was her only hope of refuge when the king's mood was so foul.

He bent down and whispered in her ear, "How can you be unhappy when I give you everything?"

She felt the rough scaliness of his hand as his grip tightened so his queen could only whisper, "The witch lies, sire. Who knows what mischief she wanted to cause between us?"

He wrapped her long thick braid once around her neck as he spoke, "There's a pretty little princess with a large dowry that I could have tomorrow if I wasn't tied to a worthless cow like yourself."

Once more he wrapped her braid around her swan's neck until with the tightening of the noose she spoke no more. The queen went limp in his arms and he discarded her like a child would a damaged toy.

He ignored Malika's kicking at the stall door and dragging his serpent tail behind him left his queen alone with her favorite.

It was hours later before the queen regained consciousness. She staggered up from the straw and tenderly touched the raw soreness around her throat.

As the king's actions replayed in her head, Elaine

started to search frantically among the stable bins and shelves for things she could use. She gathered a pile together: saddle bags, a horse blanket, two knives of different sizes, brush and comb, apples and grain.

Queen Elaine had never been allowed to saddle or bridle her own horse but she had seen it done many times. Malika stood calmly, letting her patient obedience to Elaine's fumbling at the buckles be her only response to the queen's desire for flight.

The two slipped away just a few hours before dawn, when the world still remained sleepy. Malika followed behind the queen through the formal gardens, passing between tall sculptured bushes and hedges. Their feet and hooves crunched lightly as they made their way down the winding gravel paths.

Only later did Elaine wonder why they met no one. Was it luck or her desperate prayers? Whichever, she was eternally thankful to whatever forces kept their retreat unnoticed.

The gardens led to open lawns which Elaine rushed across, fearing discovery. Ultimately they came upon the dry moat that had served as a method of defense during more turbulent times. Horse and woman stumbled down the steep bank before climbing back up the other side.

At times the queen struggled, the heavy skirts of her court attire impeding her progress. After a fall, she had to scramble on all fours to get out of the ditch.

Her fingers dug into the soil, breaking her nails, as she pulled herself up by grabbing rocks and dried clumps of tall grass.

Malika followed behind, needing no encouragement. They both knew they had to escape.

They traveled open fields until they came to an ancient forest. Using a fallen tree log, Elaine struggled to mount her horse. She was sore and stiff as well as cold.

She did not collect the reins but let the horse have her head. Malika took a gentle but steady pace, finding a path through the underbrush and trees. Exhausted, Elaine felt her head nodding to the mare's walking rhythm and soon her eyes closed.

Only when the sun started to set did Malika stop her distance-eating pace. Waking up with a start, Elaine absentmindedly patted the mare's neck as she looked around her.

Being deep in the forest, Elaine had no idea how far they had traveled. Holding onto the saddle she slid down and when the soles of her slippers hit the ground clutched at her horse to stay upright. Her legs felt strange and numb from being in the saddle for so long.

The queen rested her forehead against the horse's shoulder for a moment to collect herself. Then, she loosened the girth on the saddle and slipped the bridle off of Malika's head. She wiped the bit clean before hooking it over a tree branch.

Malika had brought her to where a large tree had grown strangely sideways; the bent trunk made a broad flat platform. Elaine pulled off the rolled horse blanket she had buckled behind the saddle's cantle. Wrapping it tightly around her she staggered over to the tree and crawled into its natural bower.

The queen, without her king, fell easily into a peaceful sleep.

Elaine slept the day and night away. The second morning she awoke to the sound of men's voices. At first, she hid under the blanket until she realized the noise was some distance away and was not coming closer.

Curiosity aroused, she left her shelter to sneak through the underbrush and discovered two men standing on the bank of a small river. One was shabbily dressed, holding a line with three large fish. The second man was better garbed, wearing the traditional brown and green livery of a warden. He was shouting at the first.

"Bunker, I've warned you not once but twice to stop fishing this river. It's under protection until we can get the fish to return."

"They've returned already!" Bunker held up his trophy high as evidence but his jest was met with a warning.

"How would your wife and children feel about seeing you in the pillory again?"

Before Elaine could retreat back behind a tree, the man named Bunker saw her and pointed. "Let this lady decide my fate."

The warden turned, and under their joint stares, the queen decided to take bold action so stepped forward. "I'm sure I could settle this argument peacefully for you both."

The warden had dealings with the nobility and he immediately recognized the queen's higher social status from the fine quality of her dress, the cultured tone of her voice, and her upright, proud posture. He bowed low and agreed that her ladyship could decide this scoundrel's fate.

"Before I can settle this disagreement though I do ask one boon," began Queen Elaine.

"Anything," agreed Bunker, performing a flamboyant, though not graceful, bow. He felt a woman would not rule against him; women had soft hearts.

"Let us cook one of these fish," replied the lady. Before either man could protest her stomach made an audible growl.

The warden and Bunker built a small fire of coals on the river's bank. Behind Elaine's back, Bunker looked a question at the warden who shook his head sharply in a negative.

Whatever the reason this strange woman had for wandering the woods alone, she was of a class that would not appreciate any demands for information.

When the queen returned from gathering herbs, both men were busy. Bunker was stripping green twigs to hold the fish above the coals and the warden was rooting in his satchel for clapbread made of barley.

As the fish cooked, Elaine questioned them both to gain a better idea of their families, backgrounds and duties. When the warden pulled the fish off the low fire, he divided it into three unequal portions, giving the lady the largest piece.

"Now, this is a feast fit for a king!" cried Bunker. So quickly did he eat his portion that the poacher had to wave a hand in front of his mouth to cool it.

The queen used the clapbread in place of a trencher and ate the trout's white flesh at a more decorous pace. One point Elaine had to disagree with was that food at the king's table had never tasted so good.

When they had finished their meal both men were in a pleasant state of mind, long past their earlier rancor. At her call to attention, they wiped the grease off their hands in the grass and sat cross-legged in front of her, ready to hear Queen Elaine's verdict.

"We know our friend, Bunker, did illegally take three fish from a stream protected by our friend,

Warden Smithfield." Elaine indicated the two intact fish and what remained of the third. "The warden protects the river so it can stay healthy for it supplies good water and food for everyone, beast and man. However, we must also acknowledge that a man must eat."

Both men nodded, agreeing with the case she was setting forth.

"All three fish are now dead, one eaten. We cannot put back what has been lost." The warden frowned thinking upon how he had just eaten a poached fish. The queen ignored his expression and continued. "A parley between warring parties cannot be accepted until we share salt and bread. Thus, one fish was sacrificed to keep the peace.

"However, to satisfy the law, we use the second." Elaine took one of the two remaining fish and handed it back to the warden. "This one shall be given to the poor so even though his life was taken through ill intent, his flesh will be transformed through a good deed."

"And the last," Elaine pointing towards the one still laying in the grass, "shall go home with Bunker. Not as theft but as payment. For his punishment, Bunker must spend the next seven days assisting the warden in learning about the river. It will be your task, Warden Smithfield, to show him why the river requires prudent care not foolish conduct."

Bunker sighed. It was a wise justice. Warden Smithfield nodded too. He needed the community to understand the value of his work and Bunker, while a poacher, was well-liked by others.

Finished, Elaine stood up and dusted leaves and twigs off her court dress.

"Now gentle sirs," she told them, "I need to find a kind woman who might provide me with a few things to continue my journey."

The men leapt up, eager to be of help to such a beautiful and kind lady. They gave her so many suggestions she had to hold up her hands and call a halt to their speech.

"One at a time, please! I have only two ears."

Thus, the queen gave her first verdict.

Queen Elaine bridled her horse, tucking Malika's black forelock under the browband.

"Malika, when did you get this white star on your forehead?"

"I've always had it," lied the mare.

Continuing her journey, Elaine followed the course of the river until arriving at a bridge. From there, she turned the direction Bunker and Smithfield promised would bring her to a friendly croft. They traveled up and down gently rolling hills until Elaine spotted farmhouses with whitewashed stone walls and thatched roofs.

As they drew closer, the sound of squabbling voices grew louder.

"It is not my fault you forgot to pen up your ducks, wench," cried a red-faced farmer. He held a wooden hay rake and gestured with it to emphasize his words.

"Now it's my fault your dog decided he wanted goose for dinner?" countered a woman wearing an apron as wide as a winding sheet wrapped about her brown homespun dress.

As the two argued, a tall, lanky youth stood off to the side, shuffling from foot to foot. The boy suddenly spoke, joining his voice with the disharmonious choir.

"How could he be faulted for chasing something that flapped and ran? He's not made to sit in a barnyard. It's hunter instincts he has!"

At the boy's side lay a large hairy dog covered with wet and mud. He stared off into the distance as if the discussion did not concern him. However, a few white feathers stuck to his coat belied his innocence.

Malika and the queen stopped on the road, patiently waiting for the trio blocking the path to move. The goodwife cried out, pointing at her, "Ask this lady here! Would you want a savage dog around you?"

The two male faces turned and looked up expectantly at Elaine. It seemed she would be settling yet another quarrel.

"I will only give you my opinion if it is over a meal," said the queen, as hours had passed since she had eaten the trout. "I have it from the warden that Agnes, if this be you," she indicated the woman with a nod of her head, "is the best cook on this road."

"Warden? You be speaking of Warden Smithfield?"

Being nearsighted, the woman came closer. Seeing the rich raiment Elaine wore, the horse's gear with decorations of silver plate, and the refined breeding of the palfrey, she bobbed in respect.

"Come up to the house, m'lady. I have something that would suit you fine."

"Wait a moment," cried the farmer, as he lay his hay rake against a low stone wall. "If we are going to abide by this noblewoman's judgment then I shall bring something to the table from my own house. I have a round of cheese, untouched."

"That would be most welcomed," Elaine graciously agreed before the woman could object. "Bring the dog in question but perhaps, this close to the farmyard we might want him on a tether...?"

Being a nice summer day, they all sat around a rough wooden table with benches situated under an apple tree. Malika's tack was stripped off and she was allowed to graze the green grass of the front yard.

"May I care for her?" the youth asked, marveling at how the horse stayed near without restraint. The queen nodded, telling him he could use the brush and comb in her saddlebags. She did not mention she had used them on her own hair that very morning.

"How lucky you came on my baking day, m'lady," said the goody.

She cut the queen a thick slice of apple tart and placed it on a wooden trencher. Slices of apple, figs and raisins oozed out from between the layers of crust. After taking one delicious bite, Queen Elaine agreed with Warden Smithfield about the goodwife's abilities.

The farmer, with his arms crossed, protested. "Buttering you up, so you'll take her side. Very unfair."

To show she played no favorites, the queen took a generous wedge from the cheese wheel the farmer had brought. Under Elaine's encouraging smile, the goodwife cut another slice of the apple tart and placed it not as gently in front of the farmer.

The queen cleared her throat and began her investigation by saying, "Tell me more of this dog."

The boy spoke first. His voice was muffled as he was bent over to pick out Malika's hooves. "Showed up like they do, whining at the door."

The farmer added, "Figured he had to be someone's but no one claimed him."

"Not a farm dog," said the woman, shaking her head disapprovingly.

"No, he is not," agreed Elaine. The dog's breeding

was obvious to her for she had seen many of his type around the castle. "He is a dog that hunts the large game at his master's side and lays at the fireside of a noble house at day's end. You cannot expect a wolfhound to be a shepherd."

The goodwife protested. "He may be noble and all that, m'lady, but that doesn't bring back my goose!"

There was a moment of grim silence as the goodwife, farmer, and boy thought of the goose. He had been fattening for a fine holiday dinner that now would never happen.

The dog's leash had been tied around a leg of the bench where the queen sat. During the meal, the hound had wiggled about, placing his muzzle into her lap. Discovering Elaine was someone who knew how to rub a dog's ears properly, he closed his eyes blissfully.

"I wonder," Elaine said, looking down to her lap, "if perhaps I could buy this troublesome wolfhound from you? Of course," she hurried on, "the price must be enough to compensate you for your lost bird."

Surprised, the trio exchanged looks.

"I think he would be a good friend for me to have on this journey," continued Elaine, already feeling the comfort of having such a protector at her side. He would be someone loyal only to her, to sleep at her feet and guard her bedside. At court, she had never had such.

"If you want him," said the man rather doubtfully. The woman was more enthusiastic about the idea. "He's quite taken with you as we all can see."

"I still think we need a dog," argued the boy. He had finished caring for Malika and was pounding the brush against the tree trunk to knock out the dirt.

"We'll buy a pup," said the farmer, who was the boy's father. "They have to be brought up, side by side, with the animals they protect to know what to do."

All was quickly settled between them. In payment, Elaine handed them a small round pearl that was from the necklace the king had broken when he had strangled her.

Thus, the queen gave her second judgment.

The pearl was a generous payment for a no-good hound and both the farmer and Agnes felt a bit of guilt over accepting it. They soothed their scruples by supplying Elaine with the rest of the cheese wheel, the remains of the apple tart, a sack full of bread, as well as a surplus of apples and grain for her and her horse.

After a night in the goodwife's bed, Queen Elaine waved her new friends goodbye and set forth again on her journey. The wolfhound seemed to know he had a new owner for with a whistle he ran after them, settling into a lope beside the queen and her horse.

"Now, Malika," Elaine told her favorite as they trotted down the road, "you might excuse away a white star on your brow, but when did you have four white stockings?"

"I've always had them, my queen," lied the mare.

The town of Riverton was surrounded by a stockade of timber with a wood gate. It was not as grand an entrance as Queen Elaine's castle with its stone walls, metal portcullis, and dry moat.

The queen had arrived on market day so there was a large group waiting to be authorized by the guards to enter the town. The excitement of doing something different, such as waiting in line, soon became tedious so Elaine looked around seeking amusement.

She noticed a nervous dark-haired woman behind her and farther back saw several rough men with unfriendly eyes staring at her. From her superior perch on Malika's back, and a wolfhound at her side, the queen felt her own situation held protection so asked the woman, "Would you like to enter with us? You can keep me company as we wait."

The stranger gave a quick nod and stepped up to stand beside Malika's stirrup. At first she was careful of the dog but the wolfhound took her as a friend and nudged his head under her dark brown hand. She couldn't resist stroking his soft fur as she told the queen her name was Bernardita.

She was a foreigner who had journeyed to the queen's domain with her husband. He was a traveling knight of no lord's household and had recently died.

"Not from the plague, my lady, never fear that," Bernardita hastily reassured her. "It was the bloody flux."

His horse and gear had been sold to pay off their debts, leaving Bernardita with what she carried on her back. She hoped to improve her fortune in town.

The queen was eager to hear about the foreign lands Bernardita and her husband had visited during their wanderings. Her new companion's colorful stories helped to pass the time.

As the line moved them closer to the gate, an argument erupted between a trio of guards inspecting a wagon and the man driving it. The wagon driver was a merchant and his cargo of stacked canvas bundles had attracted the attention of the guards.

The altercation became heated as the guards pulled parcels down, using daggers to cut the stitched cording that held them tight. As lovely bolts of fabric were exposed, Elaine gave an audible gasp at their rich beauty. She edged Malika closer for a better look.

"You are damaging my goods, you brutes," complained the merchant. He climbed down from his perch. Commanding the young boys to remain on board, he handed up the reins.

"Complain to the reeve," shot back a guard causing some that knew of the reeve's reputation to laugh.

One of the guards pulled out a length of dark wool and draped it around his body, stroking the fabric with a very dirty hand. The action so angered the merchant that he tried to grab the material but the guards gave him a vicious shove causing Queen Elaine to fear for the man's safety.

In the long tedious winter at the castle she had seen what happened when fighting men, too long without real occupation, used pride and boredom as a reason to turn a small quarrel into a fight.

The merchant continued to protest, waving a piece of paper at the officers.

"I have a writ from the king."

Scratching the bristles of his beard, the leader of the guards replied, "Too bad no one here can read it."

"I can read it," piped up Elaine. She brought Malika forward and positioned herself between the merchant and guards.

"A woman who reads?" said the bearded guard in wonder, looking at Elaine as if she was a performing bear.

Their leader ignored his sally and snapped the documents out of the hands of the merchant. He passed them up to the lady who, dressed in expensive finery, with a horse and dog of excellent breeding, might have such an eccentric skill. He knew he didn't.

Elaine opened the folded papers and scanned them with a furrowed brow. She could read only a few words but her court knowledge helped her to decipher the rest. What the merchant claimed was true for at the bottom was her husband's mark.

"This is the king's." The queen turned the papers so the guards could see where she pointed at the heavy wax seal with the dragon stamp. "These goods are destined for court. I hope the merchant doesn't won't need to explain why they are so dirty."

The guards exchanged looks at her last comment. The king's court was far away and many wanted it to remain that way. The leader of the trio snapped at the merchant, "Collect your things and stop wasting our day."

Bernardita hurried forward to help the merchant and his two young apprentices fold up the canvas bundles. They were not neatly re-tied, for everyone was in haste.

Their task was not helped by the wolfhound. Thinking a new game had begun, he barked and leapt about, getting himself entangled under the legs of the apprentices.

Elaine begged them to put the dog up in the wagon. Once the hound gained a perch where he could supervise, the chore was quickly finished.

Once in town, Elaine and Bernardita followed the merchant to his home. When his wife learned about the trouble at the gate she insisted that the women stay for supper. The merchant brought out a bottle of wine and even allowed the apprentices a small sip before he sent them off to their beds.

Queen Elaine had left the king's court wearing her evening attire and had already thought on how to fund a new life. Her girdle was embroidered with the new glass beads from Italy, her rings all held gemstones, and the necklace broken during the king's assault supplied a handful of pearls to barter.

The only dilemma was how to convert these items without getting herself reported, arrested, or robbed? Being a mere woman, it would be unusual for her to conduct such business and Elaine was not so foolish to think her actions wouldn't arouse the interest of dishonest men.

Thinking of Bernardita's predicament, Elaine explained to the merchant that she was also a widow, cast out by her husband's family. She wondered if he could possibly help her as he had the connections and knowledge, as well as the good nature and honesty to do well by her.

Eager to return a favor, the merchant agreed and Elaine thanked her good fortune.

The girdle and pearls he would broker for her though it may take time to find someone with the money to pay what they were worth. The rings and her hair pins, if she no longer cared for them, could be sold far more easily.

Tucked deep in her saddlebags was her crown but Queen Elaine had forgotten it, so never mentioned it.

In planning her future, the queen's idea to open a small bakery met the merchant's approval. Although not common, being a baker was acceptable as women's work and with the proper patron, like himself, it would not cause an uproar.

Bernardita brought more practical knowledge to the venture. It was she who picked out a location near a brewer. She knew they could use the skimmings off the froth of fermenting ale to develop their yeast.

Still, even with Bernardita's help, Elaine had many failures in the beginning. However, the queen's reserve of converted wealth sustained them while they learned their trade.

The fine pandemain bread Queen Elaine remembered eating at the King Everard's table was made from the highest quality wheat. However, in pricing the thrice-sifted high quality flour Elaine discovered pandemain was too costly for her small bakery.

Instead, Elaine bought a coarser flour, a blend of wheat, rye, and barley to make the affordable loaves of wastel and cocket. They added nuts, dried fruit and spices to loaves to provide more fancy fare for merchants entertaining.

Her new friends proved invaluable in making her venture a success. Elaine bought butter from the goodwife Agnes whose advice she often sought when the oven fire decided to burn one side of the bread, while leaving the other raw.

From Warden Smithfield she learned of a spring whose water tasted as sweet as flowers. With the help of the farmer and his wagon she hauled barrels of it to her shop.

More importantly, as the months and seasons passed, Elaine learned she didn't have to brace herself each time a stranger appeared at their door. Bernardita discovered the stability of a home.

Word spread about the odd little bakery, tucked down the least-traveled lane of the town. But it was something more than tarts and loaves of bread that brought people by for long visits, for the queen had earned a reputation for solving people's problems.

Elaine bought her flour from Odo Mueller who operated the king's mill located lower down the river. He was a broad, stout man and he came to visit her one evening after her shop had closed for the day.

Sitting at her bench near the hearth fire, Odo was either tongue tied due to the complexity of his problem or because of the beauty of the queen.

Elaine handed him a tankard of fine ale and encouraged him to come to the point.

"Come now, Odo, what is troubling you?"

It had been a long day for Elaine and she was a little tired. She was still getting used to standing all day without respite and her feet hurt.

From under her dress skirts, the long legs of Godwin the wolfhound could be seen. She had named him "good friend" since he never left her side.

"It's the reeve, my lady. But I don't think you can really help me…" He made as if to rise but the queen laid out a hand indicating he should stay.

"I've heard about him from others. He seems rather an unprincipled man."

"A what?"

"A man up to no good," explained Elaine.

"Sure that he is. I have sent my banality, my payment, to the king as always in fine pandemain flour. Now I'm told by the king's chamberlain I am short. That what they received is of the poorest quality. I filled those bags myself and I know the difference between eight from twelve even if I am a simple man."

Under the warmth of the ale, Odo's grievance became warmer. He explained that last month he had sent his tithe to the king as usual. From the wheat he milled, he had marked the bags set aside to go down the river by the canal boat to the court. The reeve had come as usual, counted and recorded the sacks as they were loaded onto the barge.

"Next I know, one of the king's men is at my doorstep. He brought a sample of the flour he claims I shipped them. It was coarse, my lady, not the fine wheat flour I had sent. It held bits of rye and barley."

Odo lifted his right hand, showing the broad spatula of his "miller's thumb" gained from years of sifting and feeling the grains of wheat in the grindstone.

"I know how flour feels. This was wrong. And it smelled wrong too. Musty and old. When I looked at the sack, I saw none of my mark even though the chamberlain insisted this was one of the bags I had sent."

Queen Elaine leaned back on her stool. Her face fell into shadow as she asked, "Do you think someone played a trick on the king?"

"Someone did something," Odo insisted. "I don't want to accuse anyone without proof but I'm sending out another shipment to the king tomorrow. If that goes awry, my head won't be worth a broken penny."

Elaine folded her hands together to stop them from trembling. She did not like the idea of being this close to the king's business. On the other hand, Odo Mueller's life was in danger if the king believed he had been cheated.

From the doorway where she was leaning against

the wall and listening, Bernardita spoke up.

"The reeve's only daughter seeks to marry a knight. That would be quite a rise in status if she accomplished the feat."

When they both looked her way, the older woman shrugged, holding her hands outward.

"From experience I can tell you that a knight will not marry a girl without a dowry. I even had such when my lord married me."

Elaine frowned. "He must have exchanged the flour but what would be the benefit of the reeve having pandemain? How could he sell it when no one here can afford to buy it? Even we can't afford to buy it."

The miller wiped his mouth as Bernardita refilled his mug.

"There are some fine lords and ladies coming through Riverton next month. They've been making a progress down the river on their way to the king's court. They could buy it."

"The church sets a very fine table," suggested Bernardita. "When the bishops come through on their travels."

"Enough with speculation," said the queen. "We need proof."

That was how Queen Elaine found herself in small alley behind the reeve's house. Mueller and Bernardita has protested, but Elaine insisted. She ran a bakery so wouldn't she be interested in buying pandemain?

She was accompanied by Bernardita because her friend did not want her undertaking such a dangerous errand alone. Bernardita did not think even Godwin was as good a protector as herself.

To the reeve's man, Elaine explained she had been commissioned to make bread and cake for a noble party coming through Riverton. The miller had nothing she could afford for such fine people but she had heard Jeffrey Reeve might have some surplus to sell her.

When the man did not seem forthcoming, Bernardita suggestively jiggled the money pouch hanging from the cord around her waist.

"He might have something," the man suddenly remembered, eyeing the bag. "But I'll need to check with him first."

The two women patiently waited while he did so. He did not return. Instead it was the reeve himself who opened the back door and ushered the two women inside.

"My lady baker and her friend," he greeted them, stroking the front of his tunic down over his ample belly.

Elaine was surprised to see the reeve's garments were finer then she would have supposed for a man of his station. It lent a bit of credence to the notion he had more coin then perhaps honest means would allow.

Elaine explained again what she sought and was twice surprised. He quickly confessed to having what she needed.

"White flour, pure and fine. Three times ground. I'm sure pandemain made from it would make a royal mouth water." While he talked, he had lit a tallow candle and was leading them down to the cellar of the house. There he showed them what he had available.

The sack he opened for them to examine the flour had Odo Mueller's mark as he had described it.

"That will do nicely," agreed Elaine.

They haggled over price and the queen lamented she had forgotten to bring her own bag to hold the flour. The reeve, seeing the coins in Bernardita's fingers, generously offered the use of one of his own.

"No extra fee. We can scoop what you need right into it," he offered. Picking up a less full sack, still with Mueller's mark, he filled it to the level Elaine indicated she needed.

Queen Elaine felt better knowing that Jeffrey Reeve was not only a thief but not a very good one. His vanity and stupidity would have caused him to be caught by King Everard soon enough. She was actually doing the reeve a favor discovering his avarice before the king.

She handed off the marked sack to Odo Mueller

and told him that it was up to him to deal with Jeffrey's duplicity. Elaine suggested that he talk to the reeve privately, letting him know that the next step would be to bring it to the king.

"He would be a fool to let this be brought before King Everard," said the king's wife.

The miller readily agreed because everyone knew that King Everard had a short temper and being a thief himself, hated any thievery not done toward his own gain.

Elaine didn't know how things were eventually settled but since Odo didn't return to her shop and she heard nothing more about it, she assumed his conversation with the reeve went well.

However, it was this judgment that returned the queen to the king's attention.

When Sir Reginald walked into the little bakery located at the end of a crooked lane in Riverton he saw Queen Elaine behind the counter and fainted.

"Oh dear," cried Elaine and called to her assistant. "Get a wet towel, Bernardita!"

When Sir Reginald awoke, he wondered if he was dreaming. Several of his fantasies of being in the queen's arms had been of this nature. Who else had that dark honey-gold hair, eyes as blue as a robin's egg, and dimples so rarely seen?

His head was in the queen's lap and she was

exclaiming over his hurts, tenderly bathing his face. In Elaine's distraction, she hastily dabbed his forehead and mouth, a process that only transferred the blood from his split lip to an area between his bushy eyebrows. Looking up at her in wonder he asked, "Can it really be you?"

"I'm afraid it is," replied Elaine, smiling. "Let's get you off this floor."

He eagerly took the hand Elaine held out to help him to rise. After standing he did not let it go.

"I didn't know… because… you must leave, quickly," the knight told her urgently. His garbled speech made little sense.

Bernardita had been cautiously watching the reunion from the doorway and Elaine turned to her friend and explained.

"An old friend from the past. Why don't you watch the counter while we exchange gossip over a bowl of soup."

Elaine brought the knight to the back of the building where she sat him down in front of the hearth fire. Bemused, Sir Reginald watched as the queen puttered around the room like an ordinary goodwife. It took consuming an entire bowl of soup before he was able to assemble enough of his wits to explain.

"The king is on his way and will be here no later than tomorrow. He is meeting a delegation on neutral ground to discuss a…" the knight continued as if riding at the forefront of a valiant charge to his death, "…marriage."

Elaine took the bowl from Sir Reginald's limp hand and handed him a tankard of ale as she replied sarcastically, "Let me guess, to a fresh, young princess that has a very large dowry? There's no reason why he need know I'm alive. He can marry this girl, poor soul. I'll not interfere."

"You don't understand," protested Sir Reginald, realizing he had not fully explained why she needed to run. "He will find out you are here. He commanded that I bring the owner of this bakery to him. Word of what you've been doing here has reached him."

Queen Elaine had suggested the two go for a gallop outside of town to discuss privately what she should do. After collecting his own horse from the inn, Sir Reginald met the queen at the merchant's stable where Malika was kept.

"This is Malika?" the knight asked in surprise, eyeing the dapple-gray mare.

"Of course it is," reassured the queen. "Don't you recognize my favorite?"

The knight was relieved when Malika's sentence, "Sir Reginald lov…" was cut off as the queen slid the bridle's bit into her mouth.

Sir Reginald watched in befuddlement as the queen

competently saddled and bridled her own horse. Perhaps this was why he was too slow in giving his hands for her to mount. She was down the lane by the time the knight had mounted.

The wolfhound ran after them both. Passing Sir Reginald, the dog snarled to remind him it was he, Godwin, who had a rightful place at the lady's side, not the knight's.

As they left through the gate, the guards gave the couple a friendly wave.

Feeling his horse underneath him, Sir Reginald quickly recovered his equilibrium. It was his dearest wish to protect the queen but it had been something he had never been able to achieve at court. His former lack now made him more determined than ever to see to her safety.

When he had accidentally discovered her, he had not demanded she immediately return to court. Instead, his advice had been for Elaine to flee as fast and far as she was able.

Queen Elaine had always thought him loyal only to the king so his care for her now made her re-think that estimation.

His dubbing ceremony at age twenty-one had been the year she arrived at King Everard's court to be wed. Yet, somehow, she had always perceived him as much older than herself. Perhaps it was because some of his youth had been spent in a monastery giving his face a more serious bearing than others his age.

Sir Reginald now told her what happened after her disappearance. The king never explained it. One day she was there, the next she and her horse, Malika, were gone. Some feared he had killed her while others guessed she had run away.

King Everard ignored his courtier's speculations and refused to send out search parties to discover her whereabouts. He handed away her clothes and jewelry to his women while he grew meaner and more vicious. Without the queen to take the whims of his temper, anyone caught in his path, whether noble or servant, was served with blows and beatings.

The king's habitual disappearances at the full moon grew longer until now he vanished for weeks, sending the court into confusion. Those with the means and connections found reasons for leaving.

"I was thinking of departing soon myself… but," he stopped, looking away from her to gaze across the fields freshly planted for spring. The queen did not notice Sir Reginald's distraction but mused out loud, "So the king heard of my justice?"

"Words on the wind came to him about a dispute over flour. Talk of a baker dispensing a law more just and wise than his own. I was sent to bring her to him so she could answer for such an affront."

The queen grimaced and said, "His pride is as fierce as his temper. What did he intend to do with me?"

"He wants to match wits against you. In truth, he wants to destroy you. Preferably in front of a large audience."

The queen gave a harsh, brittle laugh that cracked both their hearts.

"The same old game as always? He wants to appear big, while others are made to appear small."

She kicked Malika into a gallop and shouted over her shoulder at Sir Reginald, "I'm done running. If the king wants a taste of my justice, he shall have it."

Sir Reginald returned to the king's encampment, now less than half a day's journey from Riverton. He brought a carefully worded message that would appeal to his vanity.

"The baker is a simple woman and her skill, I daresay, was much exaggerated in these tales we heard," Sir Reginald informed the king and his court.

Everard smiled, glad to hear his knight alleviate his suspicions. He had heard rumors of some dispute between the reeve of Riverton and the miller which had been mysteriously resolved. The matter should have been under his dominion, heard openly at court, enriching his coffers with the compulsory bribes. He had grown quite angry upon hearing the whispered gossip.

His knight continued, "She settles trivial matters:

family disputes, squabbles over who a girl should marry, or the best age for a son to take over his father's trade. She truly is not worth of Your Majesty's notice."

King Everard was seated on his throne chair (having insisted that it be brought in its own wagon) under the awning of his splendid pavilion. Rugs, carpets and cushions made it a place where his courtiers could sprawl around him at a much lower level.

One of the few courtiers who had remained made a rude jest about the baker. Sir Reginald waited for the laughter to die down before making a suggestion.

"I heard the town council wants to build a new bridge. However there is much argument over where it should span the river. This would be an ideal test to show your wisdom to everyone at Riverton, Your Majesty."

Interested, the king leaned forward and asked him to explain the problem further. Sir Reginald told the king all that he knew about the matter. Queen Elaine had told him to hold nothing back.

She played fair, unlike the king.

The king gave orders that he would meet the baker as a combatant in the matter one day later at the location of the dispute. The day was fair and gentle when they met on opposite sides of the river.

When the king and his courtiers arrived they

remained on the opposite bank, outside of the town's boundaries.

On the town side, the lady baker waited, mounted on a gleaming white horse with a wolfhound at her side. To her left and right stood town folk who had come to be entertained by the event.

King Everard reined his bay stallion alongside Sir Reginald. He told his knight the woman must be uncommonly ugly to wear such a heavy cloak and hood during such mild weather.

Sir Reginald replied truthfully, "Undoubtedly, her face would shock you, Your Majesty."

"Fine breeding on that horse and hound though," muttered the king, frowning.

He turned his stallion about in a tight circle to again face the river. In a loud ringing voice that could be heard by all he commanded, "Let me hear the arguments for and against this bridge."

At his request, the town's people started shouting.

"Here the river is too wide."

"A bridge would open the south gate. I have land here that would prosper."

"The current is too treacherous."

"This would give a short road to meet the king's highway."

In such rulings, Queen Elaine knew the king's opinion was formed by only one thing: whoever gave him the most money. Elaine had no doubt how the king would rule as greed was his dearest companion.

Indeed, she had already learned from her merchant friend that some in town who owned property near the river had taken gold to the king's encampment just yesterday.

When the arguments, complaints, and advantages started to be repeated, King Everard rose up in his stirrups. Holding out both hands overhead, he commanded silence before he spoke his judgment.

"My opinion is for the bridge to be built here. Trade is the life's blood of a town."

The king's statement was greeted with applause from his court, however most on the queen's side of the river remained silent. As one, they turned their eyes to the heavily cloaked figure sitting on a white horse whose dainty muzzle could fit into the hands of a child.

The queen held up her hand and only the wind dared to speak.

"A bridge built here would not serve the town," Queen Elaine said in a voice that grew louder with each word.

Hearing her, the king's skin grew green with anger. Those closest to him edged their horses away.

"First, the river is a natural barrier against invasion. A bridge would eliminate this defense. Second, the silt from building it would slow the river's course, affecting the speed of the miller's waterwheel."

"Even if all that was not a consideration," continued Queen Elaine, her voice now loud and confident, "the river here is treacherous. The current is dangerous and the bottom sinks from under your feet. It would kill any who tried to cross it. Many men would drown in the attempt to build a bridge here."

"Does a woman know more than her king?!" raged King Everard.

"An honest queen knows more truth than a corrupt king! A man that tried to murder his wife!"

Queen Elaine threw back the cloak's hood to reveal her distinctive honey-gold hair and on her brow - her crown, the only thing remaining from her marriage to a monster. She had never thought to wear it again, telling herself she would only do so if she could bear its weight.

Seeing her, the king's wrath exploded. He spurred his war stallion forward to cross the river. His only thought to wring her neck again.

Sensing peril, his horse shied from the wet muddy bank, refusing to enter the fast current. Jerking on the reins, the king circled his steed back to the shoreline. But again, the horse refused.

The king, his skin green and scaly, his eyes yellow with slitted pupils, whipped and spurred the horse without mercy. The horse's ribs became bloody and his mouth a wet foam. Left without a choice, the horse plunged into the deep, treacherous waters.

As the queen's truthful sentence departed from her lips, Malika suddenly reared. Surprised, Elaine fell off, landing unceremoniously on the ground. Godwin barked excitedly, nipping at Malika's heels, and Bernardita rushed forward to help the queen rise.

Malika's white coat blazed as bright as a star and a horn of pearl spiraled out from her forehead like a newly drawn sword. Her hooves became cloven as her full tail thickened like a rope into a lion's tail.

When the unicorn spoke it was like a choir of angels sang and the notes rang clearer than any church bell.

"The queen has spoken truth. And I am her champion."

So swiftly did all these events take place, that when the unicorn sprang into the river's water she met the king's horse at mid-crossing. The unicorn struck the horse shoulder-to-shoulder and a thunderous clap sounded under the clear skies.

The force of the blow sent the struggling horse slipping sideways for as the queen had said, the river's bottom was treacherous. The current quickly submerged him, his forelegs striking the sky.

Yet even as the stallion was lost, rising from the turbulent water, crested a disgusting and vile serpent. A horrible thing of green and black scales, as big and powerful as a bull, it rose higher and higher.

People on both sides of the river shrank back from

the shoreline in fear, horses screamed in panic, and Queen Elaine saw Sir Reginald cross himself.

The serpent's thick tail wrapped around the unicorn's body, squeezing her hard even as she stabbed it with her pearly sword. With each blow of the unicorn's horn, a shrieking tore the air and with each successful strike, the unicorn's brilliance increased.

Eventually so brightly did the unicorn glow, many onlookers had to cover their eyes or be burned by her radiance. Only two were able to witness all of the battle: Queen Elaine, with her hand wrapped around Bernardita's waist for comfort, and Sir Reginald, who grimly watched the execution of justice.

Water that churned wildly ultimately grew still.

Muddy brown became red.

No living being stepped forth onto either shore. In the water was no sign of the queen's husband or her favorite. Only the body of the king's dead horse remained as evidence any battle had taken place.

Slowly Sir Reginald dismounted and reverently descended to his left knee. Through tears, Queen Elaine watched what remained of the court take to their knees. They held the obeisance due her for the required five heartbeats.

As she was finally given the mantle due her, Queen Elaine's only regret was the loss of her favorite.

The Prince
Learns a Lesson

The prince was a spoiled brat and everyone in the kingdom knew it. Nannies, tutors, royal advisers, and a deployment in the military had all failed to remedy his behavior.

Flummoxed, the king decided to place an advertisement for help in the local newspaper. Scrolling through the classifieds on her tablet, Vivian saw his plea for help while eating her morning toast.

She thought taming a prince couldn't be more of challenge than her last job. Considering the state of her bank balance it was worth a shot.

She called her grandmother for her thoughts on the matter.

"Nana, you've raised seven boys who all became good citizens. What do you think the prince needs?"

"He needs to know the value of a hard day's work," her grandmother replied loudly, so as to be heard over the noise in the background.

Vivian asked cautiously, "Do you have me on speaker phone? I told you not to do that again, Nana."

"Hi pumpkin!" her grandfather called out a greeting while Nana added, "Today is bread making day and you caught me right in the middle of kneading. What else was I supposed to do?"

"Well, I'll let you go…"

"Stop by tonight. It's potluck."

Making no promises, Vivian said goodbye and ended the call. She tossed her bathroom robe onto her messy bed and finished getting dressed.

Vivian was on the way to the subway station when she decided to call her mother for advice.

"Mother, you raised three fine girls. Why are we not arrogant like the prince?"

Her mother was standing outside the door of her yoga studio and students were already arriving. She had picked up because it was her daughter. However, she did not consider the bratty prince an emergency so replied impatiently.

"The prince needs someone to teach him his place. His father may hold the title of King, but he doesn't rule us. He's only a figurehead. The prince is just another citizen."

Vivian was about to ask for more specific details when her mother told her, "Oh honey, I've got to get this class started. Talk later."

After lunch, Vivian decided to call her aunt, her father's sister.

"Aunt Miranda, tell me why your kids are so much better behaved than the prince?"

Aunt Miranda did not have false modesty: she knew her niece spoke the truth. Awards and accolades had followed both of them from their first kindergarten scribble to their post-doctorate thesis.

Her son was a physician working for the Doctors Without Borders program. Her daughter was a pro-bono lawyer, dedicated to protecting civil rights.

"Well, Viv, it comes down to kindness. You must have a gentle heart that truly knows others. I'm sure if the prince would just understand how much he hurts other people by his actions, he would be very sorry."

Vivian, thinking of the many tabloid stories detailing the prince's exploits, felt doubtful.

"True change comes only from within. Don't you think I'm right?" her aunt asked. "What did your grandmother and mother say?"

"How did you know I called them?"

Her comment was met with a cackle of laughter from the other end of the line.

"Are you coming to your Nana's potluck tonight? We can all discuss it together."

As the advertisement requested, Vivian showed up at the king's brownstone early the next morning. It was a four-story townhouse located in an expensive district which Vivian had never visited.

It was a long block of brownstones where all the windows had a small arch across the top like a skeptical eyebrow. Each floor boasted a bow window but layers of drapes blocked any view inside, as if the bed covers were drawn up and the house was sleeping.

She trotted up the concrete steps to stand in front of a pair of heavily carved wooden doors. Vivian smoothed her hair and was about to knock when the door opened revealing an elderly man dressed in the old-fashioned servant colors of black and white.

The butler welcomed her in without asking her name. He brought her through to the entryway where the white and black marble floor continued the formal theme. As they walked down the hall way, paintings of rich people frowned down upon them.

The servant eventually brought her to a room where she was told to wait. It was richly furnished with polished antiques, dark velvets, and with a taste that proclaimed it as a sedately stately home.

Vivian wondered if she dared to sit on any of the furniture or if their delicate old legs would collapse from under her.

"Everyone has given up," explained the servant mournfully to her question about why there were no other job applicants. "After the queen's death he was five and was spoiled. Twenty years later and everyone knows it's a hopeless case."

Vivian liked a challenge. She especially enjoyed accomplishing things others thought impossible so the servant's words did not dull her enthusiasm.

"Is he really that bad?" she asked the man as he was leaving.

At her question, he looked back and said, "Perfectly horrid!" before firmly shutting the door.

The king was much like his photos that appeared in glossy magazine spreads. He had a large domed forehead with hair more white than black, and a bony nose with a long jaw, all courtesy of the lineage of his noble ancestors.

"I thought..." he began and Vivian helpfully supplied the adjectives he might be thinking.

"Taller, broader, fatter, smaller?"

"Older," he decided firmly, taking a seat.

Since it wasn't a throne, Vivian felt no hesitation in taking the companion chair, even though no one had invited her to do so. As her mother had said, the monarchy's right of rule had long been dissolved.

"I'm the answer to your problem."

Vivian felt she needed to convince the king she was the right person to do the job. She worked hard to project an air of complete confidence and competence.

"Indeed?" The king raised skeptical eyebrows but gestured with a long fingered hand for her to continue. She was the only applicant to have responded.

"If you give me three days, I will teach him three lessons that will make him a better prince, a humble man, and a loving son."

"Lessons? You do know that he came down from University without completing a semester, let alone a degree?"

Vivian gave a broad smile, her white teeth flashing against her dark brown skin. Undeterred, she outlined her plan.

"Now, Your Majesty, the three lessons he will learn are: the value of a hard day's work, humility for his station in life, and empathy for his fellow man."

The king laughed and didn't stop for quite a few minutes. While he guffawed, Vivian's smile on her face became somewhat frozen.

Eventually though, the king wiped a tear from his eye and replied, "You can have as much control over him as you desire for three days as long as you don't kill or maim him."

"Physically, he will be the same at the end of the three days as he was on the first," reassured Vivian, knowing that the king truly loved his wayward son. Affection notwithstanding, if the king had loved him less, the prince wouldn't have been so spoiled.

"Why do you think you can perform this miracle, young lady?"

"I've consulted with the three wise witches of Greenville," she told him.

Hearing this, the king felt reassured. Possibly, this strange girl with her pixie face and laughing eyes did have some credentials to accomplish such an impossible task.

"So what will be the price for this transformation?" he asked cynically.

"My boon is a simple one - all of my student debt to be paid, in full."

The king looked appalled at her suggestion.

"The interest too?"

"All of it," she insisted.

He put his hand on his chin, asking with some trepidation, "What is the current interest rate nowadays?"

She told him and he grew white and rubbed a hand over his eyes. He looked around the room and moistened his lips before stating wearily, "I have no choice. Change him in three days and I will meet your price."

The prince woke up in the form of a little pony on the first morning of the three days that the King had given Vivian. He made an adorable pony. He had a long yellow forelock that covered his soft brown eyes and a gorgeous thick tail of gold that dragged the ground.

His pony self was being led by a young woman with hazel eyes, dark brown skin, and black hair. She brought him around the corner of a very grand house that looked faintly familiar - as things do in dreams.

But while he thought it dream-like, it soon became all too real.

The pony-prince walked through an open gate into the backyard where his arrival was greeted with roars of delight by about a dozen children, all under the age of ten. Their shouting made his pony-self anxious and he tried to hide behind the girl's long legs.

"Me first!"

"No, me first!"

"I'm the birthday boy!" stated an exceedingly repellent brat - a blond child with an arrogant sneer on his young lips. The birthday boy roughly grabbed the reins out of the girl's hand and jerked the pony around so he could mount.

Unlike actions in real dreams, the harsh pull on the

reins connected to the bit in his mouth hurt the pony-prince.

When the boy plopped down in the saddle, his heavy weight hurt the pony's back.

An adult stepped forward and offered some gentle advice on how to treat the little horse. The rider was offended. He kicked his mount in the ribs with his hard heels and as they trotted away shouted, "I know how to ride. Don't tell me how to do it."

The boy rode the pony-prince all over the grassy lawn. He did not care that some people were sitting on blankets on the ground; he rode through their picnic setting. Sometimes the pony's footing slipped on cake and sandwiches or his tiny hooves broke expensive dinner-ware.

All of these rude actions caused the boy to laugh loudly and kick the pony to a faster trot. It didn't take long for everyone to learn to just stay out of his way.

Other children begged for rides too. He ignored them.

"I'm the birthday boy, not you!" He told them, explaining his privileged greed.

He seemed never to tire in his need to be moving. However, ponies, carrying a boy too heavy for them, are not as tireless. Eventually, the pony-prince stopped, his sides sweaty, exhausted.

"Bad pony! I'm your rider and you must obey me!"

His rider leaned over and broke off a twig from a

bush to punish what he perceived as laziness.

A part of the pony-prince wondered why he didn't throw the boy off and be done with such a nightmare. Whenever this thought crossed his mind, he would see the brown-skinned, black-haired, hazel-eyed girl watching him. Across the lawn, she would shake her head in the negative and the pony-prince found he could do nothing but obey.

When he heard the call for birthday cake, the pony-prince hoped he might finally have a respite but it was not to be.

"I need a sword! A sword to cut the cake!" shouted the boy.

Swatting his mount with his switch, he forced the pony-prince over to the grand table.

The three-tiered cake was a work of many hours. It had a fanciful elaborate design on the side showing children playing at different games. Large piped flowers in rainbow colors were on every level.

The party table held stacks of crystal, fine china, bouquets of flowers in silver vases, as well as silver-plate forks and stacks of linen napkins. An ice sculpture of a swan was slowly melting onto the large silver platter that displayed it.

"I'm a knight of old on my mighty steed. How can I cut the cake without a sword?" the boy pouted.

Seeing a smaller boy standing nearby playing with a plastic baseball bat, the birthday boy demanded he hand it to him. Before the toddler could comply, the repellent brat knocked the young child down and seized the bat triumphantly.

Waving it over his head, he yelled, "Charge!" and rode the pony back to the table. He battered the cake to pieces, sending frosting and cake bits flying, crashing plates and shattering crystal.

The swan was beheaded.

"Stop him! Stop him!" cried the pony-prince, "Why won't anyone stop this brat?"

But no one did. Instead the audience of adults applauded and clapped. But the children, the boy's would-be playmates hung back, hiding behind their guardians' legs.

It was only when the servants arrived carrying presents that the birthday boy dismounted. He threw away the reins away and ran off to throw himself on top of the mound of gift-wrapped boxes.

In a moment, the girl was again at the pony-prince's side, leading him away. Under the shade of a tree, she took the heavily ornamented bridle off his head. She braided his thick forelock exposing his big brown eyes.

"I should have thrown that holy terror off my back. Right into a prickly bush," the pony-prince grumbled.

"Is that how you remember it happening?" asked the girl.

"Remember what?" he asked the conductor of his nightmare.

"Your ninth birthday party? I didn't read in the *Tattle-Tale* that you got thrown off - just that you and your guests enjoyed cake on the lawn of your father's most lavish estate."

"I wasn't that - that - little tyrant - monster - horror," he sputtered, protesting.

She removed the saddle and its blanket and used a soft brush on his coat. It felt so good that he leaned into the pressure, resting his body against her.

"Why am I so tired?" he asked, his eyes blinking and head sagging.

"I think," the girl said after a pause, "that was probably the very first time you've ever put in a day's work."

"A day's work!? More like a *week's* work having to haul that little barbarian around."

"Some days do feel like weeks when your boss is so mean."

"Damn right," huffed the pony. "That kid is the one who needed a birch twig swatted on his bottom. Not me."

"But their love gave him everything he ever wanted."

"That was a stupid idea," snapped the pony-prince in reply.

"Do you think so?"

"Well, look at him! The mess he's made. The trouble he caused. Someone should have stopped him long before things got to such a pass."

"Perhaps," she suggested very meekly, "he could have stopped himself?"

"A brat like him? Not bloody likely," the prince muttered darkly.

The girl handed him a crumpled piece of birthday cake that she had found on the ground. He paused, sniffing it, before delicately lipping her offering.

It really was quite good.

Feeling mollified, he took a bigger bite before asking, "Did I do well?"

"You did," she reassured him while braiding his mane with flowers.

"You did very well, my prince."

The second day when the prince woke up, he was a mouse in the girl's pocket. She reached down and gave him a cracker and a cube of cheese.

"We shall have a long day so you might want to keep some back," she cautioned as he nibbled on his treats, holding the cracker with ridiculously tiny paws.

They rode the subway, something the prince had never done. There were a lot of people packed together and the machine rocked, squealing and shrieking as it tore down its tracks. When the cars raced through the tunnel, the noise hurt the prince's ears.

He burrowed deeper into her coat pocket, finding a haven in a sweet smelling handkerchief.

"We will be there soon," Vivian reassured him.

From the subway station, she walked several blocks until they reached a large skyscraper, its huge plate glass windows revealing only exterior reflections of sky, traffic, and other buildings.

"I'm here for an appointment at the *Tattle-Tale*," Vivian informed the officer at the front desk. His bored eyes barely saw her as he scanned her with his security wand.

As they boarded the elevator, the prince squeaked, "*Tattle-Tale*? That rag? Why are we going there?"

"For the scoop of the century," she told him.

"They print nothing but lies."

"So those photos of you, rumpled, half-naked with that actress were posed?"

The mouse-prince grew smaller in her pocket; he had forgotten about those photos.

Entering the offices of the tabloid newspaper, the *Tattle-Tale*, they passed rows of desks where reporters sat, either staring at computer screens for inspiration or talking on phones. Some seemed to be in an attitude of prayer.

Vivian came to a stop at the end of the hall where a door's nameplate boasted "Editor."

"About time you got here," the man inside exclaimed as a greeting.

He was middle-aged with skinny arms and legs, but with a large pot belly. Much like a spider, thought the mouse-prince.

"Bobby told me you were the best or I wouldn't go outside with a freelancer. This tip is so hot it's going to scorch the earth when it hits the front page."

"Front page?" Vivian repeated as she leaned over the desk to take the large manila envelope he was handing her.

The phone rang so instead of answering her, the *Tattle-Tale* editor waved her away and picked up his phone to take the call. He shouted after her retreating back, "Don't come back until you have the whole story! I'll need some proof!"

The old lady cracked open the door but the chain prevented any entry.

"Do you have the money? They said you would."

When Vivian agreed she had it, the chain was unlatched but the woman continued being suspicious.

"You don't look like a reporter. You look like some college kid."

"I'm both," Vivian agreed, "for today anyway."

She was invited to sit down in a faded living room crowded with furniture and knick-knacks that would have done a garage-sale proud. Between the smell of damp and the heavy window drapes, the atmosphere was one of slow suffocation.

The woman reached out for the envelope Vivian carried but the girl leaned back, removing it from her grasp.

"First, we talk."

She wasn't offered any tea or a drink so Vivian pulled out a notepad from her bag, clicking her pen. The pad sat on her crossed knee preventing the other from seeing what Vivian was writing.

The mouse-prince poked his nose out from her pocket. Seeing the old woman sitting across from them, he asked her, "Why are we talking to my old nanny? She's a doddering fool."

Ignoring him, she addressed the old woman.

"Tell me about when you were employed by the king."

"Are you going to write it all down in that little notebook of yours?" the old lady asked in an excited rush.

"The important bits," the black-haired girl agreed complacently. "The *Tattle-Tale* keeps your name completely private of course. We never reveal our sources."

"Except in court," snickered the mouse-prince from the cave of her coat pocket. However, his humor was short-lived for when the nanny began her story he began to gnaw angrily on his cracker with impotent rage.

"There was definitely something fishy between the king and the queen. I saw from the first day of my employment. They had a too-polite way of talking, not just because servants were in the room, but a stiff, almost formal way like they were strangers.

"Not like a man and wife at all. Their lack of relations was common gossip among us servants so I don't know why it hasn't been published before."

"Out of respect for the queen?" The old woman ignored the girl's polite suggestion and continued. She gave Vivian a knowing wink thinking she might have missed her prior insinuation.

"They weren't on intimate terms if you catch my meaning."

"That's all very interesting, however, I don't think it's worth this," the girl replied as she patted the fat envelope laying beside her on the cushion.

Standing up, Vivian made as if to leave. Reaching forward with a shaking hand, the old woman burst out, "She told me. The queen told me. The prince wasn't the king's. She had an affair. The king was a proper cuckold."

Vivian threw the envelope on the table, where it hit a stack of old copies of the *Tattle-Tale*, making them slide to the floor in a heap. The woman scrambled for the packet of money at the girl's feet.

"This is an exclusive," Vivian said loftily. "If you

take the money, you can't reveal this information to anyone else. You'll be cursed and the Tattle will sue you for everything you own."

"Oh, I won't," promised the old woman sealing the contract as she fanned the bills to better admire the large denominations.

Once out of the house, the mouse ran up Vivian's arm. He hid himself in the curtain of her black hair and nervously wiped his wet eyes with his ridiculous paws.

"That woman never cared for me," he told her in a mouse-small voice.

"She cares only for herself. It is why she will fall and break her hip on her icy sidewalk on January 12th of the next year. So mote it be."

Vivian pronounced judgment and without looking back, continued her journey.

Their next stop required a taxi. When they pulled up to the grand estate which was now managed by the government, the mouse-prince was puzzled.

"This old pile?" he scoffed. "Are we going to gape at the bed hangings that old George the 12th once used?"

It seemed there was no need to join the public tour queuing up at the side door. Vivian showed the guide a card from the king and they were admitted to the private areas of the house not seen by lowly tourists.

"I'm here to view the portrait hall please."

An old family retainer was summoned to conduct her. He was a chatty man, with a round, friendly face. He was very knowledgeable about the furniture, the rugs, and the hunting trophies on the wall. And gave the visitors a running commentary about it all as they made their way up two flights of the grand staircase.

The portrait gallery was a long grand hall that connected two wings of the palace. There were many portraits by grand masters but Vivian, not being an art major, didn't pay much attention to them.

Amongst the antiquated generations of nobility, she eventually found what she was looking for: the twin portraits of this generation's king and queen.

"So young," she murmured to the mouse-prince.

"He took his title when he was just four years older than I am now," said the mouse-prince very quietly.

He was riding on her hand and she lifted him up so he could take in the full-length, life-sized portrait of the king. It was the first time he had really noticed it.

The king's portrait showed a tall, thin man much as he was today, however in the painting his hair was dark and full. He wore an expensively tailored business suit of dark navy that displayed the light blue sash across his chest to advantage. A group of medals hung on his coat's breast pocket, more historical decoration then perhaps true trophies.

Perhaps his youth at the time would account for his

father's stiffness and the far-away look in his gaze.

"His blue eyes look sad and vulnerable," said Vivian, voicing the mouse-prince's thought aloud.

Vivian stepped over to view the companion portrait done by the same artist. The queen's painting revealed a woman in a full ball gown with long white gloves. Her tawny hair was dressed high and mounded so to best display an ornate tiara, heavily encrusted with diamonds.

She had a more sensitive face; a mouth highly-strung as if she was barely holding back powerful feelings. Such was the fire in her blue eyes you wondered if perhaps she had slapped the painter afterward.

"People say I look like her."

"Perhaps," she replied, "in the mouth, I think. But your brown eyes are not her's. Nor the king's."

Their tour guide gazed at the paintings and sighed.

"They really should be hanging at Parliament but the king keeps them here. Sentimental he is. His Majesty comes at least once a month to sit here, sometimes for hours, just to see them. He loves her still. Probably why he's never married again."

"They are beautiful works of art," agreed the girl. Even she could admire the artistry of the painted drapery, the depth of color, and the luminous flesh of the subjects.

"Both were done by David Brothers."

The retainer continued, thinking he knew all the facts.

"You might not know him being so young, miss, but he was the rage twenty-odd years back. He would have been a grand master if he hadn't died in that plane crash at the time."

He pointed at one corner of the king's portrait where there was a cascade of painted drapery. Bringing out a magnifying glass he invited her to use it to examine the brushwork.

"Because of his death, he didn't finish His Majesty's portrait. One of his assistants did this - the drapes are almost, but not as good, as Brothers'."

Their last stop was back at the *Tattle-Tale*. In their newspaper morgue, the location where all the old editions were stored, Vivian's pass got her access to a computer.

Seated, she spread out her purse and notebook. Reaching into her pocket, she invited the mouse-prince out and placed him where he could sit on top of the lid of her iced coffee, next to the computer screen.

Vivian searched the newspaper's database, going back to two years prior to the prince's birth. As she scanned through the society pages, images of the queen being escorted to various social events opened on the screen.

In photographs she often appeared cross, frowning at impromptu photographers. In posed formal shots, she seemed bored and stiff. None of them showed the fire found in her official portrait.

As the girl scanned through additional months, soon more celebrity photos appeared. In these photos the queen appeared more relaxed, with a natural smile.

In each she had the same companion. His back was always to the camera so all that could be seen was his white-blond hair.

Finally, Vivian found an article about the portrait painter, David Brothers. It was an expansive, glowing review of his work and was published right about the time he was working on the twin royal portraits.

The photo spread showed him standing in his studio, in front of easels, some half-finished. In one photograph, the background had the portrait of the queen, though it did not reveal the original's glory.

The mouse-prince felt an immediate loathing for his arrogant chin, which David Brothers liked to tip up and to the side when the camera shutter snapped.

"He photographs well, don't you think?" the girl said.

The mouse-prince stared at the man's face which was almost a mirror of his own and said nothing in reply.

The prince woke up as a human on the third day.

However, this fact did not rejoice him because his body felt incredibly old and tired. He thought he had the flu.

When he finally unglued his eyes, the prince discovered he was laying on cold cement. He threw off the sheets of newspaper that covered him and got a whiff of clothes that smelled like piss.

Using the brick wall beside him he pulled himself up, his body joints popping and creaking. Looking around the alley he saw no pixie's face; no girl with large, hazel eyes and a knowing look to serve as director for this waking nightmare.

No, he was alone except for his hunger. The pain of it raked at his ribs and made his belly ring like an empty well. The prince, who had never gone hungry in his entire life, wondered for a quick moment if he was dying.

He shivered in his thin cotton shirt for the morning air cut at him. Searching the pockets of his baggy pants he found no coin, paper, or food.

Absentmindedly, he shoved up his shirtsleeves to scratch his arms, revealing rows of puncture marks, fading bruises, and on his right wrist, a tattoo that he gotten when he had turned twenty-one.

Stunned at the sight of it, he stumbled away from the wall, walking blindly. His path took him out onto the sidewalks of the city where people bustled about, oblivious to his distress.

Until someone shoved into him and his shirt was soaked with hot coffee.

"Watch where you're going!"

The prince looked up to stare into his own face, to see his features fixed in a pattern of scorn. Had he ever been so young?

"Are you a statue?" demanded the doppleganger prince of his homeless self.

One of the young men following the prince quipped, "He appears just as stupid as one."

"He smells of piss and beer," another of the prince's companions complained. He drew back in revulsion, holding his nose.

"Like you did last Saturday night," laughed yet another of the men who composed the young prince's entourage. The joker socked the complainer in his arm with a playful fist.

The man who had accused him of being a statue added disdainfully, "The city needs to do something about this human trash on our streets."

The group of five young men were part of the young prince's current set of friends. The old prince knew them all. Knew their names. Had once called them his knights.

Today, though, they taunted and jeered, pelting food and trash at the old prince. Helpless, he threw up his arms to defend himself against the onslaught.

"Come on or we'll be late," the fifth companion

finally spoke.

He was the only one who had not participated in the jeering and assault. Instead, he was now pulling at the arm of the young prince, trying to get him to leave.

His name was Tim, Tim Galloway, thought the old prince as he watched the party leave. He looked down, ashamed. About his feet was the thrown trash and in the pile was a partially eaten sandwich.

Instinctively, driven by hunger, he picked it up but before he could tear back its wrapper a familiar voice stopped him.

"Perhaps I can help you?"

From his crouch, the old prince looked up to see his father. The king's outstretched hand helped him stand and guided him to a nearby bench seat.

In a daze, the old prince heard his father, the king, give instructions to a man standing at his side. It was his father's driver and after he left the king's attention was given to his son.

While the wry smile held a trace of bitterness, his father's tone was nothing but gentle. "I saw what happened when I was driving past. I feel responsible for your misfortune."

"No need to," choked out the old prince, looking down on the squashed sandwich that was now trembling in his dirty hands older than his father's.

"You think not?" asked the king. He sighed and

crossed his arms.

"You are generous. I would raise him differently if I had to do it over again. Hindsight is 20-20. At the time he seemed too small, too vulnerable to be harsh with, especially after losing his mother to cancer."

"He's not small any longer," mumbled the old prince but the king was distracted as his driver had returned. The man handed his employer a paper sack and two cups.

"Here, I hope you drink coffee. It's a good stimulant."

The king prepared the drink himself. He popped the lid off and shook in two sugar packets. After stirring and replacing the top, he handed him the cup.

From the bag, his father retrieved a fresh sandwich and unfolded the wrapper. He removed the old sandwich from his son's hands and replaced it with the new one. Without pausing to think the prince devoured the sandwich, cramming it down as fast as a three-year-old child eats cookies fresh from the oven.

Meanwhile, the king slowly savored his own coffee, looking as if sitting next to a beggar on a public street was an everyday occurrence. He took no notice of the people who were surreptitiously taking photos with their cell phones of the encounter.

When the old prince was done with the sandwich, the king handed him a spoon and a fruit cup of berries.

The boundless patience, the gentle kindness, returned a memory to the prince's mind: of his father feeding his grandmother after her stroke when they had visited her in the hospital.

Distracted by memories, the old prince hadn't noticed that the king's driver had left and returned again. Now he handed the king a large bag.

"I think this will fit you better," said the king.

He handed his son the sack. Looking inside, the old prince saw it contained a new shirt, a jacket, and pair of pants.

He felt his eyes grow wet and his throat closed. What had he done to ever deserve such kindness?

"Here is my card," the king continued as he wrote something on the back of it.

"If I remember correctly, there is a shelter two blocks down," the king pointed, "and if you present them this, I'm sure they will find a spot for you."

Before the prince could reply, his father stood up, returning his shoulders to their habitual, perfect posture, and walked away without another word.

His view grew blurry, as the prince used the back of his dirty hand to wipe his wet face.

On the fourth day, the king was surprised to find his son at his breakfast table. Not only was it an early hour of the morning for his son to be conscious but he hadn't seen the prince in months.

Starting his morning meal, the king warily watched the prince out of the corner of his eye as he buttered his toast. The boy hadn't seemed to have taken any harm. He looked much as he usually did: wearing expensive clothes with careless grace and his white-blond hair brushed back in a natural wave.

However, the king's relief was short-lived for the first words the young man said were, "I want to talk to you about my mother."

"Oh, yes, hm…" The king gave a nod to the servant to leave. As the door closed, he took a sip of his coffee before beginning, "I thought this day might come about but I was rather hoping…"

"That I wouldn't discover you weren't my father? That I was a bastard?" The prince's tone was soft but his words were hard.

"You are *not* a bastard," contradicted the king. "My name is on your birth certificate as your father, just as your mother and I agreed to. It is all set up with the lawyers. You are *my* son, in all the ways that matter to me."

"Mother…" began the prince, his eyes shining. The young man stopped to fiddle with his fork. Looking down, he noticed the tan of his strong young fingers against the clean white linen.

"Your mother was a wonderful woman who doted on you for five short years," said the king. "She was smart and talented. She had a laugh like sunshine. She loved you with every fiber of her being before she passed away."

"Because I *looked* like *him*," countered the prince, showing his anger, but not his hurt.

"You do look like David Brothers but you also look like her. The mouth, your attitude, that restless nature she had," continued the king, his voice soft for he too felt like crying.

"She loved him and love doesn't always chose where it lands. And he loved her in ways I could never give her."

"Because you're gay?"

"I see you *have* been listening at doors." The king took another sip of his beverage and finding it cold put it aside.

"I always wondered if you knew. Yes, because I prefer men to women. Your mother discovered my preference only after our marriage. Horribly unfair to her, but my parents had stopped me from telling her the truth. They were all about joining two noble lines of the old families and they weren't going to let anything stand in the way of accomplishing that. Dynastic rubbish and terribly old-fashioned considering we hold no position of state."

"But how could you...? *Care?* I mean even if... I'm another man's child," the prince ended lamely, still not daring to look at the king, his eyes burning.

"Because I love you. The first moment they let me

hold you, I loved you. I loved your mother in other ways, nonetheless they were just as deep and true. In you I see her again. Every day, I see her in you. How could I not love you?"

A few days later the prince sold off two of his three sports cars, keeping only his favorite. He abruptly ended his lease at the high-rise apartment, paid the penalty, and moved back to his father's brownstone.

A group text to his friends explained he would no longer be available for their late night carousing. He was busy with family matters and was learning statesmanship from his father.

IS THIS REALLY YOU? Three women texted him back in round-robin style.

YES IT IS REALLY ME. LOOK IN YOUR BANK ACCOUNT FOR A GOING AWAY GIFT.

For the prince, while spoiled, could also be generous to those that he cared for, even briefly.

His knights all found other princes to serve. Except for one who texted him: YOUR FATHER IS OK? HE'S NOT DYING RIGHT?

Tim Galloway was the only companion the prince kept in his life as he continued to change over the next year.

Once, a girl had told him that it was easy to be

friendly to nice people and harder to be kind to horrible people.

On January 11th he visited his old nanny's house. He shoveled her sidewalk, throwing rock salt down to dissolve the ice.

"I don't know what you are up to, young man, but you better get off my property. I've already called the police!"

She peered out, her face sandwiched between the musty window drapes and refused to answer the door at his knock. The prince placed the fruit basket at the door and gave his old nanny a friendly wave before leaving.

He didn't know if his work was enough to stop fate but he gave it from his heart and wished her well.

Vivian was reviewing the classified ad section, sipping her iced latte, when the prince sat down next to her. He ordered a black coffee and a Danish.

He wore an expensive trench coat, black leather boots, and a crisp white shirt open at the throat. His white-blond hair with all of its natural wave still fell away from his handsome face. That arrogant tilt of his chin was still the same.

But what she really noticed was that his brown eyes were no longer filled with disdain and cruel arrogance.

"Long time, no see," she told the prince with a welcoming grin.

"I figured I needed some months to clean up my messes. I even went and found that damn birthday pony!"

Vivian burst into laughter, causing the other breakfast patrons of her favorite diner-dive to shoot them nasty looks. It was a place people came to be alone, not to be subjected to noisy young people.

Her eyes gleaming with mirth, she continued to eat her bagel.

"Was it all real or just a dream?" he asked.

"Did it feel like a dream?"

At her smile and raised eyebrows he realized the witch would give him no answers, so changed subjects.

"I just enrolled at your university."

"It's not *my* university," she protested but he cut her off.

"Father has endowed a chair in your name so you might consider part of it as yours. Haven't you checked your email for the invitation to the reception?"

The bagel became a lump in her throat. She cleared it before asking, "Which department?"

"Behavioral studies of children. In the psychology department."

She gave him another of her wide grins, her eyes laughing.

"So what's your next step in cleaning up your messes?"

"Find something to do. I like art photography, probably something to do with my father." The prince had to work hard to prevent his mouth from becoming sour with bitterness but he managed to achieve it.

"Take some history courses. Learn more about how government works. Dad isn't a ruling monarch but he's involved. Follow a girl I like around until she gives me the time of day."

They locked eyes for a full minute. Vivian looked down at her watch and said, "It's 9:13 a.m. on August 7th."

A Society of
Heartless Women

I distinctly remember the first time I met the Red Rose and the White. We had just ended that ghastly year without a summer, when the skies were perpetually gloomy, and odd frosts and snows would cover the ground without warning. Looking back, it now seems to me the strange caprice of the weather was only a precursor to the peculiar events that would soon overtake us in Bath.

I have long desired to speak about the tragedy. Especially afterward when there was such wild speculation being printed in the papers.

However, Richard would have none of it. He said it would be improper, which is ludicrous. No, decorum was not the reason. In reality he feared our parents would learn he had been courting the White Rose of Bath.

For mother had a peculiar aversion to those connected to the Fae. She would have been extremely displeased to learn he had been dancing attendance on a Fae Foundling, notwithstanding that she was later murdered.

In October of 1816, I found myself standing in the Upper Rooms of Bath feeling distinctly annoyed. The service had run out of lemon and using it was the only way, my dear, to make tolerable the weak black tea for which the place was so well known.

I was wearing my favorite Spencer jacket. I recall that coat with special fondness as it was a particular shade of green that so perfectly brought out the color of my eyes. I have never been able to match it since.

Aunt Bella convinced Mother I needed to get out more amongst society so she dragged me to Bath as her companion. The real reason for our visit was Aunt wanted to play cards. Bella was an avid player and had already paid five shillings for a subscription to the card assemblies.

Her husband, William; you don't remember William? Before your time I expect. Such an old fusspot even in his youth! Forty years old, going on eighty.

Uncle William distinctly did not want to wait upon the pleasures of his wife and her gambling cronies in dull old Bath. Thus I was commandeered as companion with as little willingness as a sailor being impressed into the navy.

So there I stood with weak tea, dry biscuits, and wondering how quickly I could escape when every voice in the room stopped.

It was as if a bell had sounded.

Heads turned and I swiveled around, curious about what had captured their attentive gaze. I remember feeling not excitement but only a sense of dread.

No, give me credit for some sense! I am not looking back into the past and making a story with what I know now, my dear.

I really did feel a sense of foreboding as I watched the two most beautiful girls I have ever seen enter the hall of the Upper Assembly.

Despite the decades that have passed since their debut in Bath, I am sure you have heard accounts of their outstanding beauty. Those reports pale against the reality.

If you think I exaggerate, remember, they were both unnatural gifts from the Fae, making their beauty ethereal and unworldly.

Both girls had turned seventeen the summer past.

Despite only having three years differences in our ages, I felt positively gauche next to their glowing youth.

The Red Rose was Miranda Smalley. Her hair was of a particular mahogany hue - far more red than brown, and a deep, rich wood color. Not a fashionable color as the rage was for blond curls like my own, but the vibrant, wanton hue was too entrancing, too bold to ignore.

Her natural curling locks glowed like embers under the brilliance of the crystal chandeliers hanging over our heads. The girl's blue eyes were large and black lashed. Her mouth stained by the reddest of berries. Skin without a freckle and so pale it was as translucent as fine porcelain.

But Miss Smalley's beauty was nothing compared to the grace in which she entered a room. She glided among us like a swan, bestowing a smile upon everyone with the air of a queen.

Not one of us could have matched her in looks, style, and air, except the young woman who accompanied her.

The White Rose - what a gentle, harmless creature she was!

Do you recall her name? I see that you do not. Even history uses their titles of The Roses the poets compared them to.

Melinda Brown. Such a common name for such an

uncommon girl.

If Miss Smalley was a torch, Miss Brown was a snow-cap. Her hair was that white-blond you normally see in those of Norse heritage. It lay smooth as a dove's wing along the sides of her cheeks.

While Miranda's complexion was pale coolness, Melinda's was warmest ivory. Only when the girl blushed did the shade deepen to rosy cream.

Her full lips were the lightest tint of coral. Her large, brown eyes as dark-fringed as her friend's.

Melinda was a little shorter then Miranda but both girls were of that height that delighted men. Their necks were as long as lily stems and their slender hands were those of a painted Italian Madonna.

Naturally, two lovely girls would never go unnoticed. However, because of their Fae heritage, their presence emanated an unnatural magnetism upon the men. All of them, available or married, sought to be at the side of the two girls.

Boys of calf age or grandfathers, it did not matter.

I found this phenomenon singular and I wasn't the only one in the room who noticed their strange power. Mothers frowned in disapproval and more than one young girl's disposition showed vexation.

It was no wonder that one Fae girl was dead and another insane before the season ended.

"Who are those girls?" I asked my relative for,

though Aunt Bella was addicted to cards, she loved gossip even more. It was from her that I learned of the girls' curious histories.

The Roses were Fae Foundlings. As infants, they were discovered under rosebushes during the summer of 1799.

That was an odd year when childless mothers across England, wishing for offspring, gained their heart's desire. Babes were found in wood piles at the back of the kitchen door, under cabbage leaves in the vegetable patch, or perhaps tucked under a rose bush.

Some blamed the turning of the century for the bumper crop of Fae children. However, unlike other years when fewer Fae Foundlings were discovered, these proved to be a stunted harvest.

These Foundlings did not attain their seventh year, let alone their seventeenth. Slowly and silently, they withered away. Their deaths baffled the scientific community as no medical intervention could prevent their inevitable demise.

Eventually, only two Fae Foundlings from 1799 remained: Miranda and Melinda.

Miranda Smalley was found under a red rose bush. I was assured by her mother it was a perfectly ordinary climbing rosebush growing over the front door of the Smalley home in Wiltshire.

On the same day, in the same county (practically next door if you go by country miles) Melinda Brown was discovered crying under a white rosebush.

Neither girl competed with the other but made rather a pretty counterpoint. Miranda's voice was compared to a songbird while Melinda played the harp like an angel. Melinda painted watercolor landscapes but Miranda did only pencil and charcoal portraits. One read poetry and the other prose.

All of this I learned as the weeks passed and the year drew to a close.

That early in the season there was not much competition for company in my age group in Bath. Thus I was often in company with the Rose girls, attending the same teas, parties, and concerts.

Normally, I would have found it amusing to see men act like fools over two Fae changeling girls, but Richard, my mother's youngest, was soon amongst the number of the enchanted. Another man of my acquaintance, Mr. Hugo Trent, also succumbed to their spell.

Yes, I see you have heard of Mr. Trent.

His heartbreaking suicide a few years later is almost as well known as the Rose scandal.

There is one truth about the Red Rose and the White that history has decided to veil because of the sweet sentimentality we hold for the dead. The girls were hardened flirts, coquettes of the worst type.

No matter what the men did, the girl's hearts were

untouched. Their laughs remained gay, their smiles undiminished, and their eyes bright and clear. The men and boys that courted them were no more important to them than their last Marzipan candy.

When you accept such adoration as your due but withhold your affections, at a certain point it becomes wanton cruelty.

If the Roses had fallen in love or showed favor to one over another perhaps they would have been forgiven. But their heedless behavior, with such lack of feeling, is why the circle of eligible ladies in Bath could not forgive the Roses of their poaching.

As another more famous person has said, the society of Bath is restrictive. It is small. It is intimate.

Gossip over teacups became tempests.

It is now a well established, scientific fact the Fae have only half a heart, so together the Roses made a whole.

I've attended some of the lectures on the subject at the Royal Society in London. If you have the opportunity, do attend one of them. If you are fortunate, they will bring out their specimen jars showing the well-preserved Fae hearts no bigger than a walnut.

It truly is fascinating.

My brother, Richard, developed a passion for the

White Rose. However, being Fae, Melinda had no room in her heart for anyone but Miranda. I believe if the young women loved anyone, it was only each other.

My brother was at home making wild statements about defending a girl's honor against rogues while Mr. Trent no longer visited us.

This made the Roses a troubling personal matter.

"Something must be done," said Aunt Bella, not for the first time.

Her eyes bulged as she watched my younger brother bound up the stairs and slam his bedroom door in a fit of pique.

We had just been subject to yet another tiresome diatribe on the subject of the Red Rose and the White. My aunt gave me a meaningful look and beckoned me back into the room with her fan.

"I cannot share this news with your mother," she whispered frantically, gripping my upper arm rather tightly in her hysteria.

Aunt Bella was right about mother. My invalid parent would not be pleased to hear that Richard, the youngest and dearest to her heart, was ranting about buying a pair of dueling pistols.

I promised my Aunt I would look into the matter. She gave me a trusting look before trotting off to consult with the cook about dinner.

During the unpredictable and gloomy summer, mother had taken to her bed with a weakness of the blood. Her retreat from managing family matters had placed me in a strange position.

Being the only available female, I was suddenly in charge of matters of the heart despite my youth. Especially when it came to Richard, who was younger than myself by only one year.

I had two older brothers but there was quite a gap in our age. They were both married with families of their own for over a dozen years, so their involvement in our lives was little.

Richard and I rarely saw them so it was easy to forget their existence.

"Something must be done," said Penelope Carlisle.

Oh, how I would be heartily sick of that phrase by the end of the year!

Miss Carlisle was the type who always desired to be a leader of whatever group she joined. But she lacked the skill to organize even a scavenger hunt.

She was also the kind of heedless young woman who, when told the porridge was still too hot to eat would be the first to eat a spoonful when your back was turned.

We were at an intimate concert with tea, arranged by her mother as a private entertainment for a close circle of friends.

Since her parent had pointedly not asked the Roses, no man attended. All had sent their regrets so it was to an all-female battalion that Miss Carlisle addressed her frustration.

"We cannot compete with their beauty," pointed out Miss Hayward. She was one of the plainer girls of the group and thus could be far more blunt about the current state of affairs.

However, those that considered themselves beauties bristled at her words. Miss Simmons spoke loudly to drown out the protests.

"I for one, don't mind them having admirers. It's only natural, since they are so beautiful. However, to command *all* the available young men is too much. Not sporting of them."

You won't know Miss Simmons as she died two years later after taking a bad fall at a local hunt. Very keen on hunting was Miss Simmons. She came from a large family of many brothers and had a very loud laugh.

After more talk of what should be done, and the desperate woeful mutterings wondering *if* anything could be done, the voices finally dwindled away with no plan of action. Finally, Miss Carlisle noticed I had not contributed to the discussion.

"Is there nothing you can add?" she asked me pointedly.

I put my teacup aside and addressed them.

"It just strikes me in a curious way, why have two Foundlings survived when all of their Fae brethren did not."

At my words all heads turned toward me. When I want it, I too have a mesmerizing manner. However, I, unlike the Roses, know when to use it.

It took a full minute before Miss Simmons spoke, "Whatever do you mean?"

"Have none of you wondered what is keeping Miss Brown and Miss Smalley alive? They are not natural children, unless," here I hid a deprecating smirk under my fingertips, "you believe children are born under rosebushes."

"They aren't?" asked Miss Bunter, and the others shushed her in annoyance.

"Do none of you read?" I continued, "Peruse the papers for the latest in science and literature? The Red Rose and the White are anomalies. They should be studied by the Royal Society, not dancing away in Bath. They are curiosities. Freaks. Aberrations in nature."

Miss Carlisle may have lacked leadership qualities but she was cunning in the way some stupid women are. She later married a political man whom she helped rise to power before death in childbed ended her vocation.

It was she who asked thoughtfully, her beautiful brow furrowed, "Why do they exist, you mean?"

"Know that," I said, as I freshened my teacup (thankfully Miss Carlisle's mother made sure her household provided lemon), "and you will have your answer on how best to deal with the problem these two present."

I was not present when Miss Carlisle visited Mrs. Brown but I heard the details later. Clever Miss Carlisle made sure she paid her call when Melinda Brown was not at home.

During her visit the only thing out of the ordinary she discovered was the presence of a tiny rose bush, growing in a fragile teacup. The cup and rosebush were displayed with reverence, taking center stage on a wall shelf hung in the front parlor.

This petite horticultural wonder was about the size of a lady's closed hand. The plant boasted a profusion of white blooms, each absolute perfection in miniature. None of the roses were bigger than the nail on Miss Carlisle's pinkie.

"How lovely!" commented Miss Carlisle who walked over to observe it more closely. But she quickly recoiled in disgust at the plant's putrid odor. She later insisted that it smelled of the grave, but I do think we can put that down to girlish excitement.

Before anything more could be said or done, Mrs. Brown took her visitor by the arm and steered her away from the fascinating rose bush. Miss Carlisle was ushered quietly, but firmly, out of the door.

Informed by Miss Carlisle of her discovery, a few days later I made a similar call upon Mrs. Smalley. It was Wednesday and I knew that her daughter, Miranda, was being escorted by Mr. Trent to one of the Upper Room concerts.

"My Aunt is so absentminded these days. I wondered if she left her kidskin gloves when we visited here last week?"

I knew that Mrs. Smalley, whose social sphere was quite lower than my own, would invite me in for a longer visit. My position demanded it.

During our tete-a-tete, the woman made clumsy attempts to learn the full details of my brother's inheritance. What was his income and how large was his estate? How did his prospects compare to Mr. Trent's?

This venal interest did not encourage any sympathy to grow between us; quite the opposite in fact.

I felt no reticence in explaining the full details about my younger brother's expectations.

While my father had wealth, little of it would come to Richard. Our older brothers would gain the bulk of the estate. As the youngest son he was probably destined for the clergy, especially if my mother had her wish.

Oh, her inquiries about Mr. Trent rankled me

sorely!

The Red Rose had quickly supplanted any affection he may have once held for me. My connection had been dropped in the most humiliating manner.

Mr. Trent had grown very attached to Miss Smalley. His display of interest was so obvious that the persistent rumor amongst us was Miss Smalley would accept him before the year would end.

Mrs. Smalley ignored the delicacy of my feelings to advance the objectives of her daughter. Her obtuseness made me grow quite angry though I had the good breeding not to show it in my face or manners.

She had no right to ask me to discuss the man my heart had once thought would be mine in matrimony. So I feel no blush to admit I might have overplayed the direness of Mr. Trent's circumstances.

Mr. Trent was a handsome man, I told her, with a fine leg, and was considered a talented rider. He had a town house in London and a country property in the north but I knew little more of his situation.

I reluctantly confided that the last time my carriage had driven by his Bath residence on the way to the park, I had seen the removal of furniture. Whether that was being done by a bailiff was only conjecture though there were several raised angry voices I had heard in passing.

During the conversation, my eye discreetly

wandered about the room. I eventually found it: a little teacup holding a miniature rosebush, which sported perfect tiny red blooms no bigger than the nail of my pinkie finger.

"I do hope Bath hasn't been too tiring for Miss Smalley. I seem to see her everywhere I go. Her beauty far outshines us all."

Mrs. Smalley smiled and blushed with pride.

She really was an immensely stupid woman.

My discussion with Mrs. Smalley did provide a measure of peace to our household. Richard's suit had been strongly discouraged by the girl's parents and he was being invited less and less to the Brown's functions.

However, Richard's behavior continued to be annoying. No longer was there talk of duels but plaintive moans about not being invited to attend his "perfect angel."

There was a natural lull at Christmas. Some went home to celebrate the holiday with their families, while others remained in Bath to throw elaborate parties.

For our own household, we returned to London as Aunt Bella needed to kiss her husband's cheek and replenish her bank balance. Richard, broken hearted, came with us and spent his time gaming at his club.

The trip to town provided me time to shop and

acquire things I needed. For example, I found a new pelisse trimmed in fox fur, and located a few holiday gifts for my family.

Letters from home indicated that while mother was getting no better, neither was her health worsening. I made murmurs about returning to be at her side but she wrote and insisted I serve as Aunt Bella's companion for just a bit longer.

Considering later events, I have always wondered if she regretted her insistence on the matter?

Being delayed by roads and weather, we returned to Bath after the new year. My aunt was in a jubilant mood as she read the gossip from several thick letters sent by her cronies.

"My dear, imagine this, Miss Melinda Brown has been ill for several weeks now."

I was gazing through the window of our carriage, so my Aunt probably missed seeing my lack of surprise at her news.

Ladies will always find a way to punish those who step out of line. When malicious gossip fails them, they will seek more desperate and drastic measures.

During our absence, I had been kept fully informed by numerous letters from Miss Carlisle, almost as many from Miss Simmons, and even a few from Miss Wellstone. I was not unaware of how matters stood.

Miss Carlisle had detailed an intricate plan to

humiliate the Roses. Miss Wellstone wanted to know if I thought it a good plan? Miss Simmons wondered if we weren't all rushing our fences, preparing ourselves for a bad tumble.

I did not reply but instead wrote pleasing letters about the weather, my shopping, and the holiday season. I had no intention of committing myself to a letter that could be read by just anyone.

I have always been a most careful individual.

Fashion, dresses, and hairstyles were the concerns of us ladies as the Thursday evening of the ball approached. With the dismal winter almost gone and Twelfth Night recently past, minds were hungry for gaiety and warmth.

I had known via their letters that the first fancy ball of the season was planned. The theme for the exhibition dance was *Seasons* and for the ball itself the *Herald of Spring*.

All the ladies were encouraged to wear bright and pretty colors so I had purchased in London, along with my other items, a fashionable gown of blush pink. My black Domino was re-lined in the palest shade of green.

When I removed it, it provided the illusion of a spring flower being revealed. The color suited my blond curls and cat green eyes.

The evening program included Miss Carlisle and a

select group of friends opening it with a Quadrille. Though I was begged to be a part of the dance by its performers, I politely declined.

The Quadrille was Miss Carlisle's idea and like many of her proposals was far too obvious in its intention.

It is always better to be discrete in your dislikes, my dear. Be indefinite in your preferences for another's company, or lack of it, as it keeps your social circles wider.

And it keeps you out of the courts.

The Quadrille was currently the rage since Lady Jersey introduced it to the London set. The dance had taken on a life of its own with parties adding costumes and themes as organizers all tried to outdo each other.

For this exhibition performance, instead of having sets composed of male and female partners, the group of eight would be all young ladies. The *quadrille des contredanses* would have two squares of four, Miss Carlisle leading one and Miss Simmons the other.

We arrayed ourselves at the sides of the hall to better watch the performance. The small orchestra started a short introductory tune and the performers walked forward to take their places.

They all wore soft pale colors, befitting the ball's motif and their youth. Around the brow of each girl was tied a gold ribbon and in their hair nestled a profusion of hothouse rose buds. Miss Carlisle's group had red roses; Miss Simmons, white.

Miss Carlisle had selected Miss Bunter as her partner; probably because the latter could be easily influenced and would not outshine her. As Miss Carlisle stepped forward she made a pretty step pattern of diamonds with her shoes. As leader, her form was copied in turn by the other ladies.

The Quadrille made its way through the standard forms: the *Le Pantalon*, the *L'ete'*, *La Poule*, and *La Pastourelle*.

During the music for the Shepherdess, the dance took on that ominous nature later written about in contemporary papers. However, those accounts pale next to the appalled shock felt by the audience who witnessed the events as they unfolded.

When she stepped forward, Miss Carlisle reached for a ribbon hanging at her waist. She pulled the tail of a bow and untied a small pair of scissors, much like what a dressmaker might use.

From her hair, the girl selected a red rose and using the scissors, she made a dramatic gesture of cutting the petals off one by one. The cut blossoms fluttered in shreds to the polished wood floor.

Miss Bunter, that useful idiot, copied her mentor's movement.

The ladies stepped over the fallen petals, the toes of their slippers smashing the floral remains under their soles.

All the pairs in the Quadrille did the same. Miss Simmons group selected white roses from their coiffures. These were savaged by sharp scissors, dropped to the floor, and trampled with disdain.

The orchestra continued but all conversation in the room ceased as the macabre steps to the dance continued.

Miss Melinda Brown, the White Rose, was absent from the ball, due to her continuing poor health. However, her Fae Foundling sister, Miranda Smalley, was present.

While her Fae heart may only be half, she had a full sized brain. She recognized the insult. The threat and animosity from the other ladies was no longer behind closed doors but was openly defiant.

I was standing directly opposite from her position in the hall. It was an ideal place to witness the scene that took place between her and Mr. Trent.

Miss Smalley's naturally pale complexion now took on the fixed hardness of an alabaster statue. Frigidity that intense can only be caused by the deepest anger.

It appeared Mr. Trent was trying to soothe her feelings but she would have none of it. She removed her fingers one by one from Mr. Trent's arm where they had been resting.

She turned to say something to her mother, Mrs. Smalley, who was standing at her elbow, her mouth agape in bewilderment.

The music, as if on a cue, ended. The Red Rose's ringing tones could easily be heard throughout the long hall.

"These simpering idiots think to humiliate us!"

Miss Carlisle couldn't have planned it better. Only boldness and endurance can carry you past such a mortification.

Miss Smalley, with her indiscreet words, lost the first round.

The next morning, coming down for breakfast, Richard stopped me with a hard hand on my arm.

Richard had been our escort the previous night and the carriage ride home had not been pleasant. He spent the entire ride accusing me of "pulling the strings to make my puppets dance" and other insulting insinuations.

"Did you know?" he demanded harshly, his round baby face finally showing some manly strength to it. I again denied having any involvement in the events at the ball, but he cut off my explanations.

"Miss Brown has died."

I was taken aback at his abrupt statement. I had no idea her illness was life-threatening.

"Did you not?" snarled my brother at my astonishment. "You and your little harpies are probably preening yourselves hearing the news."

Aunt Bella, who had come into the hall to see what the commotion was about, stopped the conversation with her good sense.

"Last night showed an embarrassing lack of manners by many. I'm sure those girls are being punished by their families this very morning for their reckless abandonment of decorum," Bella said.

"However, while Miss Brown's death is unfortunate, she did not die from mortification. It has nothing to do with your sister and is no concern of ours."

"We poisoned her."

At Miss Carlisle's statement, I was dumbfounded for the second time in a day.

"Surely I misunderstand you," I began. Miss Carlisle waved my statement aside with a trembling hand.

She had arrived later in the morning. Since Aunt Bella had left to pay her own calls and Richard had angrily tramped off to discover more about Miss Brown's demise, we were private.

Her incriminating words spilled out in a rush.

"After you left to London, I told the other girls about Miss Brown's rose bush."

Tears leaked from her eyes, making them a puffy, red mess. I handed her a clean handkerchief as hers was a soggy limp rag.

"I didn't know. I didn't know."

"Know what?" Under my stern eye, she gulped and took a few deep breaths before continuing.

"Each of us visited the Brown's residence. Over the next few weeks. Each time one of us visited, she put something on the rose plant."

"What a foolish thing to have done."

"Laurel Water, Camphor, Henbane… Hemlock was from Miss Simmons."

As if it mattered what poison Miss Simmons had used! I was incredulous at the level of stupidity the girls had displayed.

Not only in attempting to poison a magical rose bush but in detailing the method in which they had done it. I hoped they hadn't written about it in diaries kept tucked under pillows!

"Tell me no more."

I wondered how much I should tell her. Would it alleviate her feelings of guilt? Or should I let her continue believing she and her playmates had murdered an innocent girl?

"Do you not understand the role the rose bush played in sustaining the life of Miss Brown?"

At my query, she shrugged and sniffed into the fresh linen.

"Through blood and bone, my dear Miss Carlisle. Through blood and bone those two girls have lived to be seventeen. It's human blood and human bone that made those roses bloom. Ask yourself what lives were fed that rose bush to keep a Fae Foundling healthy for seventeen years."

By the time Miss Carlisle left, I felt the beginnings of a horrible migraine. Between gathering poisons, spilling them onto roses, and their public exhibition at the ball, those idiots had landed themselves into a right mess.

My repose was interrupted by Richard.

Rudely, he knocked at the same time he entered my boudoir. I removed the wet cloth from over my face to reveal my frown of displeasure.

He ignored my censure and sat down on the side of my bed. I covered my face again but he did not take the hint and started telling me all he had learned about town.

"Miss Smalley has been in a very public row with Mr. Trent. She's as much as accused him of murdering Miss Brown out of jealousy. She said that Miss Brown was the only one she ever loved and that Trent couldn't stand it."

I sat up in bed, the cold washcloth long discarded.

"How dare she!" I seethed, headache forgotten.

"I thought you'd want to know Trent is being attacked and for no good reason."

He crossed his arms. With Miss Brown dead, her spell had quickly faded, and it was replaced with sympathy for his fellow man still caught in the trap.

"What are you going to do about it?"

Mr. Trent's reputation took a severe blow with Miss Smalley's public accusation.

It should have been ludicrous to accuse him of killing a young girl in order to win the affections of another. But his obsession with the Fae Foundling had been so devout and vocal it caused many to believe the incrimination.

Like all ill-natured gossip, it left a stain on the person who had vented the accusation as well as the object of it. Between the public row with Mr. Trent and the harsh degradation she had been subjected to at the ball, Miss Miranda Smalley found herself desperately in need of friends.

The next day over breakfast, the butler brought me the calling cards from Miss Smalley and her mother. I wondered out loud if I should pay them a visit, causing Aunt Bella to contribute her wisdom.

"I don't care how beautiful she is," began my aunt, her frown stopping my brother Richard from speaking what was on his own lips, "the girl lacks common sense. As does her mother."

"None of this would have come to such a pass if those two girls had shown some restraint. Your lovely sister is just as handsome and talented but you don't see her making a cake of herself."

I laughed lightly, setting aside my breakfast toast

uneaten.

"Surely, Aunt, you cannot blame Miss Brown for her own death. Whatever the cause of her illness - and let us be reminded that the doctors still have not come to a conclusion - being ardently admired wouldn't have caused it."

Richard spoke up, contradicting me.

"I think you underestimate the level of animosity those girls have towards Miss Brown and Miss Smalley."

I certainly did not underestimate it but I was not going to share with my family what Miss Carlisle had confided to me.

I thoughtfully rubbed my thumb over the cream colored cards.

"All the more reason for us to show kindness to Miss Smalley. I think I shall call on her today."

The mischief done by Miss Carlisle and her friends had spun far beyond their ability to control.

As Miss Simmons would have said, the horse had the bit between its teeth and was set on a gallop. All a rider could do was hold on for dear life.

My stroll through town had been stopped several times by others quick to tell me the gossip. Prattle had multiplied and become extremely vicious.

These tales were not about Mr. Trent but about the two girls. With the mysterious death of Miss Brown, whispers were now of back street deals for body parts, buckets of blood, and grave digging.

My question to Miss Carlisle about how the Fae Foundlings possibly sustained themselves had apparently been shared. Coupled with Miss Brown's sad, but inexplicable death, the bloom was off the Roses.

I was not surprised to learn I was the Smalleys only caller for the week.

Mrs. Smalley was a stout woman. The type you might see at a country fair admiring the cattle before she moved on to view the swine. She greeted my arrival with the fervor of a recently discovered long lost relative with money.

My glance around the room was casual as I had no desire to put the Smalley's on alert as to my interest. In the Smalley residence, the petite and delicate red rose bush still held its place of honor in their front sitting room.

However, a precaution had been taken as it was now under the protective dome of a large glass cloche. The presence of the glass shield showed awareness. It made me wonder how much the Smalleys knew about Melinda Brown's death.

Despite being half-hearted, Miranda Smalley did look very sad and paler then usual. She seemed lethargic and already in a decline over the death of her friend.

I was surprised that her parents had not immediately removed her from Bath to Wiltshire. In retrospect, a change of scenery would have done her good and perhaps saved her life.

However, as I have noted before, Mrs. Smalley was an extremely stupid woman, though, admittedly, a devoted parent.

"Only when I was with Melinda did I feel like a whole person," the beauty said, her voice as limp as her spirit. Her fingers fretted with the frayed ribbons of the reticule resting in her lap.

"I miss her so."

"It is a very sad thing," agreed Melinda's mother, beseechingly looking my direction.

"It's a great loss I am sure," I commented, adding truthfully. "She was an exceptional beauty and far too young to have left this world."

She nodded sympathetically.

"I was in London over the holiday. I didn't realize the severity of Miss Brown's illness. Is there truly no idea of what occurred to cause such a fast decline?"

Mrs. Smalley's surreptitious glance towards the rose bush indicated she knew exactly what had caused it. However, out loud she said, "Not exactly. A wasting."

"Don't talk of it mother! It was evil," cried Miss Smalley. Her voice gained vigor from an infusion of ire, containing equal parts grief and anger.

"It was all done on purpose. We know by whom! His jealousy of Melinda was disgusting. His public condemnation of her was so obvious that even papa, the gentlest of men, admonished him."

"I would caution you Miss Smalley," I used a mild tone, so she would not take umbrage at my advice, "Mr. Trent could bring an action of slander against you."

"He wouldn't dare!" the girl said, showing spirit.

I marveled at her boldness but I agreed with her opinion of Mr. Trent's lack of action. He would never do it even to quiet the rumors. Not because of a lack of daring but too much feeling.

Despite it all, he still loved her.

Mrs. Smalley reached out a hand, but did not quite dare to touch me. The appendage wavered, powerless, until falling back hopelessly into her lap.

"We've been asked, officially, to attend the inquest," she began, adding in a rush, "My husband leaves to France in a fortnight on business so will not be able to accompany us. I wonder if it would be too much of an imposition to ask you to join our party and attend with us?"

Of course I agreed.

I wouldn't miss the spectacle.

Typically, a coroner's inquest is not where I spend my afternoon though I've found them vastly entertaining in the years since Miss Brown's.

Miss Brown's death was of such a peculiar nature it had gripped not only the imagination of the newspapers, but also members of Bath's highest society. We were all onlookers or bit players in the tragedy.

As Mrs. Smalley, Miss Smalley, and I arrived in my carriage we were forced to use the services of a constable to lead us through the crowd. He forced the curious to give way, but not before I heard one woman say, "There must be something in it, although I never thought it myself."

Mrs. Smalley thanked me yet again for lending my presence to her small party of two. With her husband gone, the two women were left to fend for themselves.

I thought her husband excessively rude to abandon his family in their hour of need. But perhaps Mr. Smalley did not like being involved with something so official?

Even Richard and Aunt Bella had condemned my appearance at such a vulgar event as an inquest. But I did not relay my family's feelings on the matter to Mrs. Smalley.

By agreeing to be their companion, I had gained a coveted seat. As witnesses, the Smalleys were seated on a bench, second from the front. It provided me an excellent view of where the coroner would preside over the proceedings.

The crowd was still growing and the press made the chambers quite warm. I opened my fan and slowly wafted it before my face while my eyes scanned the room.

Mr. Trent, still handsome and expensively dressed, was seated on the opposite side of the aisle. He did not acknowledge my nod and kept his eyes fixed straight ahead.

It was my first inquest. Even with my later experiences of them, the proceedings into Miss Brown's death will always hold a special place in my memory.

For as you see, it was all fresh and new. My child-like mind absorbed all the details like a first visit to the London Zoo. I was entranced and entertained, wanting to clap and boo (which other members of the audience did quite frequently) but I restrained myself.

It seemed like a play, something staged, and not real at all.

Having more than a passing interest in the latest scientific discoveries, I found the medical testimony especially interesting. It was very inconsiderate that some of it was unintelligible even though I sat on the second row.

I blame the doctor as he was a soft spoken, elderly man. The gasps and outcries from the courtroom as the audience heard the doctor's testimony did not help the acoustics either.

If you are going to attend an inquest or trial, please have some respect for your fellows.

We all want to be a part of the excitement.

Dr. Ezekiel Millstone from the Royal Society confirmed what I had once told Miss Carlisle. Melinda Brown's heart deviated significantly in size from human standard.

While a phenomenon mostly of interest to scientists and poets, the stunted heart confirmed the girl's Fae lineage. With Melinda Brown's Fae morphology scientific fact it caused some confusion as to how to proceed.

For since Miss Brown was proved to be Fae, and not human, had a crime been committed against her?

The coroner decided to first determine if the evidence indicated a crime. If so, it would later be up to the King's Court to decide whether to prosecute.

The crowd cheered upon hearing the inquest would proceed.

I was very fortunate later that afternoon to hold a few moments of private speech with Dr. Millstone.

While he was a learned man he was as timid as a rabbit. During our discourse he used his handkerchief to nervously clean his spectacles at least three times. His gaze refused to meet mine and afterward he quickly scampered away.

I do not think it presumptuous to state that our

brief exchange probably led to the paper that made him famous just ten years later. Even amongst learned circles today, whether those of the Fae lacked moral sensibility or are simply immoral is still hotly debated.

What caused some excitement was the testimony that Miss Brown had been poisoned.

While others leaned forward to hear more, I had to smother a smile on my lips. I had not seen Miss Carlisle in the audience when we entered. If she had come, had she just fainted at the doctor's testimony?

The coroner accepted death by poison as the official verdict of how she died. However, the evidence of so many *different* poisons had prevented the doctor from stating conclusively which had given the fatal blow. Or if she had taken the poisons by accident or design.

What caused the most sensation was when the doctor revealed the true mystery.

It was unknown *how* exactly the poisons had been administered to Miss Brown. For between the doctor and the magistrate no one could confirm how the girl consumed it.

Nothing had been found in the house or kitchen to account for all the poisons identified. Most of her meals were shared with others of the household, or at an entertainment with others.

There was nothing in her room or bathroom to

hint at where Miss Brown could have swallowed massive quantities of Laurel Water, Camphor, Henbane, and yes, even Hemlock.

Irritated, I murmured behind my fan, "Like calls to like, you simpletons."

Like calls to like; Miss Brown's diminutive rose bush was herself. When you fed the rose bush you sustained Miss Brown. Poison one and you have tainted the other.

It was lowering to think that even Dr. Millstone had not made the connection. Though I tried to give him the benefit of the doubt by assuming that Mrs. Brown would have disposed of the incriminating floral specimen long before his arrival.

Distressing to hear was the testimony that Mr. Hugo Trent had been Miss Melinda Brown's last visitor.

He took the stand and, dare I say, the emotional distress he had been suffering gave his face a degree of address far superior to any man in the room. The broad shoulders were shown off to advantage in his tailcoat. He had no need for shoulder pads, did Mr. Trent.

"Yes, I had tea with Miss Brown on January 24th at her home. I was concerned for her health," beside me Miss Smalley drew in her breath at his words, "and inquired after it. That was all."

He did not fare well under examination.

It seemed he had been a little too free with his tongue when at his club. He admitted to having said very unpleasant words about the girl to his acquaintances, blaming her for the lack of his suit prospering with Miss Miranda Smalley.

"I only felt that Miss Brown had an unnatural influence upon Miss Smalley," he protested but the coroner seized on his words like a terrier following a rat down its bolt hole.

"So you did blame Miss Brown for why your courting of Miss Smalley wasn't progressing?"

Mr. Trent turned a beseeching plea towards Miss Smalley but her averted gaze was all for her lap. Since we had arrived the girl had been nervously shredding the ribbons and delicate fabric of her reticule.

The coroner's next question was demanding.

"We have heard testimony here that on your last visit to her house, you begged Miss Brown's forgiveness. She denied you, did she not?"

Other witnesses did not help Mr. Trent's case.

Worst was testimony from Mrs. Brown. As a grieving mother she won much sympathy from the ladies in the gallery. She testified on how much her dear girl changed after Mr. Trent's last visit; how Melinda had retired to her bed feeling sick and never rose from it again.

She was a noisy crier and many in the room were sorely affected by a mother's grief.

The inquest exposed Mrs. Smalley to be the type that listened at keyholes. Ready to cast blame anywhere but at her own daughter's slippers, she confirmed hearing Mr. Trent talk disparaging of Melinda Brown on more than one occasion.

"He spoke wildly, trying to get my dear daughter to agree to his suit," Mrs. Smalley explained.

"When she refused him, he threatened her friend, Miss Brown. He said if it wasn't for her, my daughter would agree to marry him. His countenance frightened us so severely that Mr. Smalley forbade him the house just a week prior to Miss Brown's passing."

When Miss Miranda Smalley took the stand, the crowds were as eager as hounds who have scented the fox. Behind my seat, I heard more than one whisper, "ghoul, changeling, devil's spawn."

While I never really cared for Miss Smalley, I will not deny she went to the stand with style. Her posture was tall and erect, almost to the point of being arrogant. She answered all the questions defiantly, her voice clear enough to be heard to the very back of the room unlike the learned Dr. Millstone's.

But to those who paid close attention, there was evidence of her inner turmoil. The girl's hands opened and closed her reticule with that same nervous tension I had seen yesterday, and her habitual paleness was no longer the shade of lilies but of a corpse resting in the coffin.

Someone shouted from the back, "Ask her about the bones!"

Before it could be suppressed, more voices joined in the chorus, "— and the blood! — and the grave-robbing!"

Miss Smalley's face flushed from white to scarlet. Like at the ball, her temper got the best of her and she couldn't restrain herself when humiliated. She rashly retorted, "Those are filthy slanders!"

But at that moment her reticule, subject to her abuse, burst open, spewing its contents.

From my view in the second row, I watched as the small bones flew out and a tiny skull landed on the desk of the coroner. It rolled to a stop where his hand rested.

Her mother vehemently denied any knowledge of the small skeleton that had so dramatically made its appearance. However, the incident was too stunning, too public, and it made rumors established fact.

It was decided by public opinion that the Red Rose and the White were Fae ghouls.

The courts were in a disarray about how to proceed.

Many believed that Miss Melinda Brown had survived using foul means, just as (it was also believed) had her friend Miss Miranda Smalley. Otherwise why would a skeleton of a premature infant be carried about in Miss Smalley's reticule?

Was Miss Brown, a Fae and clearly not human by any legal definition, even a victim of a crime?

Perhaps the Fae changeling had been put down by someone who had discovered her ghoulish need for blood and bone?

Regardless, something had to be done quickly to quell the panic of the populace.

The next time I saw Miranda Smalley was at a licensed home for lunatics.

To avoid being prosecuted with the possibility of a hanging at the end of it, an agreement was reached with her and her parents that she would be confined to a private institution until her death.

I visited her several times and always brought a little present such as a bit of Marzipan, a tin of biscuits, or a fashion magazine.

While I had never cared for the girl, it was only right that she be aware of how she had arrived at such a place.

The next year, Miranda Smalley died at the private sanatorium. By that time we were in national mourning for the tragic death of Princess Caroline.

I doubt many took note of Miss Smalley's passing.

Mr. Trent was never prosecuted.

I do not believe it was the suspicion that he was

possibly a murderer, but the congratulations from his fellows on his near escape from being engaged to a ghoul which destroyed him in the end.

My brother Richard kept the connection as much as he was able. It was through him that I learned of how low Mr. Trent's moods had become.

I would have lent him my support but he still loved Miss Smalley and refused to see me.

He departed soon for Germany, in my opinion a poor choice for someone feeling depressed. Word reached us months later of his tragic suicide.

Miss Carlisle and her set were stiffly polite in all their future dealings with me.

They gained no comfort from our encounters. I said nothing of what I had been told or if I would ever reveal that information. But a smile from me and the blood would drain from their faces.

I held them all in the palm of my hand.

What most people don't seem to realize is all servants can be bribed. Gone are the days when serfs lived in terror of what their masters might do.

By bribing, I mean not only money. That is the least useful way to manipulate a servant in a rival household. No, it is far better to promise them a more advantageous position, or provide them with an opportunity for revenge upon their employers without any threat of retaliation.

Be careful, my friend, and do not make the mistake others have made of thinking servants are dumb and deaf.

The Smalley family had come to Bath with very few servants from their home. Instead they hired local staff or used servants that had come with the house they rented for the season.

This made it even easier to implement my plan for making Miss Smalley pay for her treatment of Mr. Trent.

I had long noted Miss Smalley's habit of teasing her reticule when distressed. It only took a few judicious snips of a pair of dressmaker's scissors at the seams, replacing ribbons with ones more worn, and the deed was almost guaranteed to come off.

Oh, you wonder about the skeleton? I procured it when I was in London. It's far easier to gain such specialties there than in Bath.

My parents did not like me remaining in Bath during the Rose scandal. I was bid to come home immediately.

In truth, they had no cause to worry as I am more than capable of handling my own affairs. However, to please them and put their minds at ease, I returned to our country estates by the way of London where I did one last shopping trip.

Dear Mother didn't want me placed in any danger

169

because of the silly behavior of two society misses. For I was the wished-for daughter, the one my mother had fervently prayed for and found under a holly bush.

After arriving home, my parents informed me that because of recent developments they thought it best that my own little holly bush be sent off to a nunnery.

The dears had already found one, quite remote, in eastern Europe, where the nuns (believing the holly bush a manifestation of God's divine power) would pray over it, feeding it the blood and bone it needed.

The place is so obscure that it would be a surprise if anyone other than the Pope was aware of its location.

I know I've only gone once.

Only once to see that my little holly bush flourishes like a green bay tree.

Granny Starseed

Granny Starseed arrived one month late to visit her sons and grandchildren.

"Just like your mother," grumbled Sarah to her husband, Arthur. "She hasn't visited us in years so why now?"

While Sarah spoke the truth, there was nothing to be done about his wayward mother. Arthur shrugged and continued with his morning routine of getting ready to leave for his job as president of a bank.

His wife continued airing her grievances.

"Just because we have a guest house doesn't mean your two brothers couldn't share the burden of looking after her."

By this time in her narrative Arthur was brushing his teeth. He gave her a nod, the foam in his mouth serving as an excuse for not answering.

"At least you have work and can avoid her. I'm the one stuck dealing with her."

After spitting into the sink, he told her, "She won't stay for long. She never does."

Of course Arthur loved his mother despite the trials of his childhood. But having her and his wife under adjacent roofs had proved a nightmarish land to navigate; the two were diametrically opposed in all things.

Sarah loved the insular environment of their gated community, the unofficial wife's club that met for exclusive lunches over Bloody Marys, and the elitism of driving a Lexus.

His mother, with her long white braid threaded with feathers, torn jeans splattered with paint, and her tendency to forget to wear a bra when out in public, was not part of the pretty picture Sarah wanted displayed to the world.

Later that day, the three brothers, Arthur, Osborne, and Bernard, met for a bite at a local pub to discuss the problem.

Bab Dannon had been a flower child of the 1960's and between free love and communes, half of their parentage remained unknown. Similarity in temperament and appearance though stamped them as close family.

All of the brothers were tall and large, with the broad shoulders and intimidating bulk of linebackers. Arthur, the oldest, was the biggest, Osborne almost as tall but with a more lean build, while Bernard, coming in at six foot, was the shortest of the trio.

Arthur was the wise older brother who the other two had relied upon during their turbulent childhood. He had risen quickly up the corporate ladder and was the youngest branch president of a bank.

Osborne was the comedian, always ready to make funny faces or mimic voices for a joke. Ozzy was so good with people and selling with a smile that in the last ten years he had grown his mowing business into a landscaping empire.

Bernard was the youngest and his older two siblings would never let him forget it despite his deployment to Iraq. While his brothers didn't believe working at a motorcycle shop had a future, they stayed silent on the matter as befitted their mild natures.

Appearances notwithstanding all three men were gentle giants. It was often this mildness which gained them grief from the women in their life.

"But what *is* mother doing *here*?" asked Bernard, sipping his longneck. "Her gig is usually some war-torn, third-world country, feeding refugees. Has she said?"

"Mother? Tell me something of value?" Arthur grumbled. Osborne raised his beer in a silent salute to the accuracy of the remark.

"No, she hasn't said. Just unloaded an amazing amount of junk from that ridiculously tiny car and took up squatting in our pool house."

Artie continued griping, knowing it was safe to unload to his brothers.

"Last night the fire alarm went off at two in the morning. I rushed out there, thinking the place was burning down and found all the smoke was due to mother burning incense. She was in one of her trances, oblivious to its piercing shrieks. I ended up yanking the alarm box off the wall to get it to shut up."

"I'm sure that pleased Sarah," grimaced Osborne. "How is your kid dealing with her?"

"Logan," said Arthur, referring to his eleven-year-old son, "just ignores her. There's no prejudice to it. He ignores us all."

Ozzy grabbed a handful of pretzels and popped them into his mouth one by one. He spoke around the crunching.

"Mother's restless. She'll be back to globe-trotting in no time. It has to be hard with Sarah's griping but you should just ride it out."

"Easy for you to say," countered Arthur, for his

middle brother had no wife or child at home to concern himself with.

"She'll be gone soon," agreed Bernard.

Bab Dannon was enjoying an afternoon without the irritating and hovering presence of her daughter-in-law. After complaining about Bab's car being parked in her way, Sarah had left to run errands.

Bab was hopeful she would be gone all day.

After taking her morning Skyclad swim in the backyard pool she settled down in a deck chair to read a good book. Her raven familiar Mara gave a throaty cack-cack causing her to look up to see her grandson, Logan, enter the backyard. In the two months Bab had been visiting she knew this was the wrong time of day for him to be home from his private school.

The boy dragged his backpack on the ground behind him, his slumped posture indicating grave defeat. At the back door, he fumbled with his key but before he could finish opening the door, Bab was at her grandson's side.

In a friendly, conversational tone, she asked, "What's the problem?"

"What do you care?" he snapped back. His voice as raw as his flushed face. He was a skinny boy, not quite grown into his future height, with straight black hair and pale skin that burned easily.

"I've got some pretty good chocolate chip cookies

at my place," his grandmother said.

If Logan had been a few years older he would have told the old lady to mind her own business. However, he was still young enough to desire the comfort of his elders during times of trouble.

He followed the long swaying white braid back to the pool house. It was the first time he had entered the guest house since his grandmother had taken up residence. Logan felt he had entered an exotic land.

The place looked completely different from the cool blue and white beach decor his mother had put into place. Gone were the decorative model ships, the bowls of shells brought back from vacations to Florida, and the framed shadow boxes of nautical knots displayed on the wall.

Now, there was a crazy profusion of color with tie-dyed pillows and throws covering the furniture and a dozen over-sized cushions on the floor. Some tall glass thing with a spout bubbled on the counter.

The place smelled different and it made him want to sneeze.

"This milk tastes weird."

"It's goat's milk. Drink it," his grandmother commanded as she handed him a plate with some very gooey chocolate chip cookies.

The boy eyed her over the rim of his milk glass. He wasn't sure what to make of her. To Logan's young eyes she seemed incredibly old, the oldest person he had ever met.

He only knew of her through the family story told by his father about when Logan was born. Apparently she had caused a ruckus at the hospital by insisting on taking home the afterbirth and the caul. When he asked his mother what those things were she had shushed him.

Logan pulled out the crumpled paper from his backpack and reluctantly passed over his report card. When her face remained impassive seeing the F, he figured she was too old to understand what it meant.

He condescendingly explained to her the dire consequences of getting a failed grade, ending his oratory with the less pompous statement, "Mom is going to have a cow."

"For once she would be useful," judged his grandmother who had a fondness for cattle.

Putting the paper down she walked over to a wall shelf where, finger over her lips, she carefully considered the collection. Once it had displayed his mother's collectible figurines but those were now gone and in their place were rows of colorful rocks.

Her pet raven, never far from her, flew in through the French doors and took a perch on her shoulder. The black bird was huge, almost as big as Logan's torso; the boy found him fascinating, yet intimidating.

"Cack-cack," the bird croaked, pushed his head

forward so his throat feathers fluffed out.

"Which do you think?" Bab asked him.

"Cack-cack."

Having received her answer, Bab picked out three of the stones. She laid them on the kitchen counter-top so their placement made a triangle.

Mara jumped down from her shoulder onto the counter. Even though he was just a bird, his face had a cynical, knowing look as he divided his time between looking at the rocks and Logan.

"Blue agate for communication and peace," his grandmother pointed to a pale blue, pretty stone, "Apache Tears for your youth," a black, glassy-looking rock, "and since you're a Pisces, this rainbow Fluorite will help too."

She picked up the last, a green-purple gem about the size of a robin's egg. When she turned it, prisms were displayed. After he had a chance to look them over, Bab scooped them all together and placed them a soft leather bag. She slipped the cord of the bag over Logan's neck and settled the pouch onto his chest, giving it a final, comforting pat.

The boy sighed but took the gifts. He knew his grandma was strange, but it was sad to have his mom's judgment of 'totally clueless' be confirmed. At least the cookies were good.

Bab's oldest son Arthur pulled his Audi into the

garage. As he opened his car door, his mother emerged from the shadows. He felt a degree of wariness seeing her and greeted her rather formally.

"Does that milkshake place still exist? The one we used to go to when you were a kid?"

Taking the hint he walked around the car and opened the passenger door for her. Returning to his side, he texted his wife that he was taking his mother out for a drive.

After a moment he thoughtfully added, TO GIVE YOU A BREAK.

Eating from the plastic food baskets with their red and white checkered paper caused a flood of childhood memories. All of them bad.

Such as living out of the back of their station wagon, his mother's inevitable merry-go-round of interchangeable boyfriends, being stopped and questioned by policemen, and wearing clothes pulled out from donation bins.

Arthur would have heartburn later that evening, if not from the cheap chili, then from his mother. Well, at least the milkshake was still good.

He contemplated his mother's profile as she, in turn, people-watched strangers.

If you were kind, you'd call her features handsome. The prominent nose she had passed down to all of her boys, but the deep lines bracketing her mobile mouth and the stubborn chin were her own. She seemed no older than the last time he had seen her - aged, but at the same time ageless.

"Cough it up, mother. What did you want to talk to me about?"

"Logan's in a jam at school. Got an F in German."

"Sarah won't like that," he said before he could stop himself.

"So I've heard."

His mother slurped hard on the straw; the cup was empty and the sound irritated him as much as her comment. Her next observation poured salt into a wound that had never healed.

"Everything else is A's. You certainly never brought home a report card that good."

"Did I ever go to school on a regular basis? I forget," he replied, his voice a bearish grumble. "I seem to remember taking a GED so I could get into a community college. College paid for with my two jobs, sometimes three."

"Don't regret your childhood, Arthur. You cannot cage a free spirit."

There were benefits to cages. Such as a roof over your head, food on the table, and clean clothes to wear.

"We are talking about Logan," his mother reminded him, drawing him away from his thoughts.

"My son is my business."

"That's good to hear! I thought you'd handed all of the balls to Sarah."

The white-haired woman flipped her long braid back over her shoulder and her eyes went black. Arthur ignored the warning for he had seen her in all her moods. They no longer impressed him.

"She's my wife and while I might consider your advice on how to raise my son, from a woman who let others raise her own, I won't hear a word against her."

His statement received a devilish grin in return and her eyes returned to hazel, more green than brown.

"Good. Because a man should stick up for his wife. That I can respect."

She sucked again on the milkshake's straw. Arthur reached over and removed the cup from her hands.

"Returning to Logan, he's a natural scholar. He'll be a famous poet someday, like you could have been."

"Mother, can we not go down that road again," he said tiredly.

Bab Dannon thought Arthur should have made a name for himself writing songs about fighting social injustice like Woody Guthrie. She could never understand that years of being forced to play in front of her friends like a performing monkey made him loathe the guitar.

"He's just at the age of self-doubt. What he needs is the right motivation," his mother said, rubbing her hands in glee.

"What do you have in mind? *Exactly?*"

"There's an exchange student at his school, from France. She's very cute but her English isn't so good. She probably needs someone to help her don't you think? Someone smart like Logan."

One of the many things Sarah disliked about her mother-in-law was her lack of boundaries. For example, the woman had taken to inviting people over to the pool house without even a by-your-leave. As a result, Sarah never knew when her property was going to be invaded.

This evening it looked like another impromptu party would soon be starting. Bab Dannon had staked out Tiki torches, digging out chunks from the tidy rug of well-civilized green lawn that surrounded the pool.

Two men arrived in a beat up van (*stalker van* Sarah's mind immediately labeled it). She guessed it was probably leaking oil all over her pristine driveway. From its interior they unloaded grocery sacks and picnic coolers, drums and blankets.

The fact that both men were gorgeous and shirtless, only increased her uneasiness.

It's not because one of them is black. I'm not racist. It's the tattoos.

From the extra bedroom at the back of her house she would be able to get a better view of what Bab was up to. Sarah ran up the stairs to the second floor and used her cell phone to call Arthur.

"Listen, Sarah, don't interfere. I meant to tell you about it before I left for this conference. It's the full moon in March."

"The full moon? What has that got to do with it? She's not a werewolf."

He laughed but she heard his boss, the regional director, calling his name. She sighed. She'd have to handle his mother on her own. Again.

There was nothing Bab liked better than being surrounded by strong, handsome men. Muscular shoulders, big biceps, a flat chest, and defined abs were not a treat to go unappreciated by old eyes.

The presence of their masculine energy made her feel young again. It delighted her old heart and got her root and sacral chakras humming.

"Set the drum right here, Jason," she told the black firefighter.

In the way things naturally happened to her Bab had met the Army veteran at the local natural food store. Feeling his need for healing, she had started a discussion over a pyramid of apples.

With Jason's connections to other veterans, her network grew. To welcome them all, Bab had arranged a Hero Feast for them. The celebration would also serve as a fine initiation for her grandson.

"Logan, you stay right on this pillow," she told him.

"No matter what happens you are just to sit here. Observe and record is your task and it's an important one."

Following his grandmother's directives, the boy took his journal and pencil to the cushion laid out on the grass. He flipped opened his notebook and started writing.

The group of half a dozen attendees included the two guys who had helped his granny set up her party. Jason, the firefighter, had an easy smile and an attitude that immediately made Logan feel important and confident.

Wyatt was another giant, though one with blond hair. He had a much more reserved, almost abrupt, manner. On one bicep was drawn the image of a bulldog dressed in a cap, and the other was an American flag with the initials USMC beside it.

The large mapwork of old scars on his stomach was probably why his smile was grim.

A girl with sides of her head shaved, wearing combat boots, set a soda drink, hotdog, and a bag of chips down beside Logan. She tossed him a grin before joining the group on the small lawn.

After everyone was introduced to each other, his grandmother moved them into position so they loosely formed a circle. Once they were all set in place, she walked clockwise around them, clapping her hands and chanting.

Logan didn't recognize the language so wrote down in his book: *not German, French or Spanish.*

The full moon had risen in the night sky. From where Logan sat, the glow was behind his grandmother's head, framing her white hair like a halo. The flames on the Tiki torches twisted from the breeze and made her features alien: half in shadow, half illuminated by the orange light. As she poured beer on the grass, the wind kicked up and Logan had to scramble to keep the pages down in his notebook.

"Hail, the arrival of the champion!" she cried and through the yard gate she had earlier insisted be left open, a massive dog entered.

It was a black and tan mongrel, with a thick matted coat and a blunt muzzle. It had that shy but beseeching, lost look of one who desires acceptance but expects only rejection.

"Come forward for the hero's portion," Bab encouraged him.

At her words the dog trotted to sit down in front of her. He gave a hopeful whine causing her to laugh. Bab went over to one of the tables that held food and grabbed a handful of smoked ribs. As she threw them, the dog leapt up, snatching them from the air.

He settled down next to Logan's knee and started cracking the bones.

"Now we shall dance!" his grandmother cried, and clapping again, the party started.

Logan had not been present at many adult gatherings. Usually he was sent up to bed where he'd spend the evening with his headphones on playing video games. So he wasn't sure if his grandmother's party was something usual or not.

He watched and took a copious amount of notes.

Sometimes he was uncertain of what he saw. Was it all real or just something his imagination created from the shadows?

Jason, Wyatt, and the others drummed and danced while figures multiplied behind them, making it seem like a crowd. As the humans in the circle sang, drummed and danced, the figures outside the group fed off their excitement.

The shadows grew larger, their flapping arms becoming wings.

At one point, Logan felt he was surrounded by birds, ready to be lifted up with them in flight. But no matter how hard he tried, the boy could not see the faces of those who danced in the shadows.

Next to him, granny's raven, Mara, was helping himself to the chips the boy had forgotten.

"She gives them back their courage. Experiences of war crush the spirit."

Logan frowned at what the raven had said. From his vantage point of eleven, Jason and Wyatt seemed pretty intimidating dudes to him. He wouldn't need courage if he looked like them.

The raven, cocking his head with that knowing look, hopped to Logan's knee. He tapped the point of his beak on the boy's journal.

"Write down what I said, bard."

Logan dutifully complied.

As the night continued, the music in the backyard grew louder. Sarah wondered why her neighbors hadn't already called the police but the street in front remained empty of black and whites.

She had tried to reach Arthur several times but her calls had all gone to voicemail.

She paced the house, her emotions beginning to become hysterical. Sarah always relied upon her husband to calm her down; he was her rock.

Reluctant but desperate, she called Arthur's brother Osborne. They didn't know each other well but Sarah needed reassurance.

"Just let her be," Osborne said. "I know mother's an eccentric but there's no harm to her."

"Could you come over…?" Sarah cringed at asking. She knew Osborne's landscape business meant he worked very early morning hours so she wasn't surprised when he said he wouldn't come.

"Really, it will be fine, you'll see."

Because he was tired, Ozzy's lie didn't sound convincing.

When Sarah finally realized her son wasn't in his

bedroom, but outside with that mad woman, she was pushed to take action.

While Sarah had a desire for the finer things in life, two things supplanted it: love for her husband and only child. So when she stormed out to the backyard, it was with the sincere fury of a mother bear who believed her cub in danger.

Sarah was a woman who had been taught never to show her anger; she suppressed it, funneling it into other channels she thought more acceptable. So when she finally confronted her mother-in-law it was with another topic than the one on her mind.

"Are you burning marijuana in my lobster pot?"

Bab, caught mid-laugh in a discussion with Wyatt, turned to look where Sarah was pointing.

"Don't get worked up, Sarah," Bab said soothingly. "It's not weed, only mugwort. And that's legal everywhere except Louisiana."

Seeing her son sitting on a cushion on the grass, with that black bird of Bab's and a strange and scary cur beside him, outraged Sarah further.

The dog looked uncared for, with no collar.

It probably had rabies.

"Logan get up and come with me," she commanded her son. "It's far past your bedtime."

It was spring break so bedtimes shouldn't have mattered, but Logan was feeling rather tired. He was also an obedient boy so closing his notebooks he gathered his notes.

"Bye granny," he told Bab receiving a mild "see ya later, kiddo," in response.

He hadn't reached the back door before the fight between his mother and grandmother exploded.

"You're a bad influence, Barbara."

"My name isn't Barbara," said the old woman, narrowing her eyes at her daughter-in-law's tone.

Sarah ignored her, and looking around, took in the party: the women who seemed to smirk at the interchange, and the men, disturbing in their virility.

Subliminally, she sensed there were others present she couldn't see. Out of sight, probably hiding, Sarah supposed. Criminals, druggies, or something worse, knowing Bab.

"You need to find another place to stay."

"I thought this house was paid for by my son."

"And this mutt…"

"Do not insult the one who took the Champion's portion."

Bab's voice was frosty and should have been enough of a warning but Sarah was on a rampage and spoke before thinking.

"The dog is disgusting. It looks savage. Probably diseased. I'm calling Animal Control right now. They'll most likely put it down."

Sarah had a deep seated fear of dogs from a childhood incident and brought out her cell phone as if to make the call. If she had taken a moment she would have remembered that animal control didn't work this late at night but in her anger and fear she forgot.

At that moment what had been in the shadows, swept forward. It brushed aside men and women and grabbed Logan's mother. Sarah had no time to struggle before she was thrown into the pool. Arthur's wife was a competition swimmer and should have been fine. She should have surfaced, sputtering and cursing, but instead she sunk to the bottom of the deep end.

Seeing what happened, Logan dropped his journals and ran screaming towards the pool. Bab grabbed his arm, stopping him while Jason dived into the water. In just a few strokes, the firefighter was at the spot where Sarah had sunk. Taking a deep breath he dived under. It was some moments before he re-emerged.

When he brought Sarah's limp form to the pool's edge, she wasn't breathing.

One moment Sarah was dead and the next she was breathing.

As she regained consciousness, Sarah feebly pushed against a firm masculine chest before turning aside to retch out a gallon of chlorinated pool water.

"She's fine, she's fine," Bab told Logan as he cried, his face pressed against her waist.

Sarah was never exactly fine again. Logan discovered, as his father had before him, that nothing his grandmother touched remained the same.

When Arthur returned home it was to the frightening vision of an ambulance parked in front of his house. He found his wife upstairs resting as she had refused to go to the hospital. Their son had fallen asleep in their bed, lying next to her.

"I just want to rest," Sarah told him but her words were so faint and feeble, that instead of reassuring him, it only frightened Arthur more.

He stroked her hair until she fell asleep.

Afterward he went out to have words with his mother. He found her at the pool house, trying to clean out a big red pot.

"Pack up your stuff, Mother. You can stay with Osborne."

"I didn't mean for that to happen…" She began but her oldest son curtly cut off her explanations.

"I know your handiwork. You and Sarah don't get along but I love her. I chose her as my partner because she is exactly the opposite of you. She cares for me, makes a comfortable and beautiful home, and loves our son."

As he talked, his voice grew deeper, until he was near shouting.

"Yes, she can be irritating and cares too much

about her clothes and her make-up - but Mother, really? *Really?*"

Bab sighed. She couldn't fit into her son's world and he wouldn't fit into her own.

"I'm packing. I promise. But I want you to know that I really didn't mean for anything like this to happen."

"I know, Mother. But you never do. You never do."

Though Osborne's charisma and hard work made his business successful, it would never have been truly prosperous without the organizational abilities of his office manager, Gabriela Morales.

When Arthur arrived at his brother's office he had to wait while Gabriela radioed the teams their latest agenda.

"Ozzy is out on site," Gabby explained to Osborne's eldest *hermano*. "Is something wrong?"

Arthur looked down at the woman; even wearing her tallest heels the top of her head barely came to his shoulder. He had known her for years but was suddenly aware that he didn't know if she was married, had children, or siblings.

"Do you have a mother?"

She laughed and rolled her warm brown eyes at him.

"Of course I do."

"Well…" he floundered still not sure what to say.

No one had a mother like his.

Used to dealing with Ozzy and his inability to discuss his feelings, Gabby tried to help Arthur get to the point. She had a long day ahead of her and was eager to get started.

"Ozzy told me your *mami* is in town. Are you having difficulties?"

"She's outside," Artie said abruptly. "Waiting in my car."

He would not bring her home again.

"She needs to stay with Ozzy for the time being. Perhaps you could entertain her until Ozzy gets back?"

"Baile, botella y baraja," said Gabby and at Arthur's puzzled looks she translated, "Dance, bottle and cards. Keep her busy."

"Cards might be safe as long as you don't bet against her."

Arthur's doubtful musing made Gabby laugh.

"It's just a phrase from Puerto Rico. It's about keeping her out of the way. Don't worry, I'll look after her today."

Before he left, Arthur warned Gabriela to be careful.

When Bab Dannon entered the office of her second son, Gabriela Morales was talking in Spanish on the phone. She waved Bab over to take a seat on the couch. After she ended her call she stepped around the desk to shake the hand of her employer's mother.

Gabby was professionally dressed in a dark navy skirt, soft white blouse, and black heels. Her makeup and nails were immaculate and her naturally wavy black hair just barely touched her shoulders.

"So nice to meet you, Ms. Dannon," Gabby said. "Ozzy won't be back until late in the afternoon. He's meeting with an apartment management team about taking over all of their landscaping. That's over 28 properties."

"That's fine. I know my appearance was unexpected. Perhaps with Ozzy gone we two can take off for an early lunch together?"

Thinking of all she should be doing, Gabriela's smile became a little frozen as she explained, "I usually eat at my desk."

"Oh, I think today is far too nice to stay inside, don't you? I have a few errands to run today and Artie told me you could help with that."

As they exited the office building, a large shaggy dog, with a matted filthy coat came up to them, wagging his tail. He sat down next to Bab's leg and the woman stroked the top of the dog's head.

"He's my guest," explained Ozzy's mother. Before Gabby could digest it, a large black bird landed on

Bab's shoulder. The raven cocked his head inquisitively at Gabby.

"This one your's?"

"Yes."

Gabby fished in her purse and withdrew a different set of keys than the ones she had initially retrieved. The company truck had signs advertising the business on the doors but it was used to mud, dirt, and chaos. With its quad doors and back seat it would be a better choice for her companions than her sedan with its leather seats.

"Do you like Tex-Mex?"

When Bab agreed, Gabby took them all to her cousin's restaurant. It had outdoor seating with patio tables and umbrellas.

It would allow a bit of the rank doggy smell to dissipate.

Over their early lunch, Gabby felt it her duty to inform Osborne's mother about how proud she should be of her son. As Bab Dannon listened she fed soft tacos to the dog that lay at her feet.

Gabby told Bab about Ozzy's hard work and dedication, the big contracts he had landed, how much their income had increased over this year, as well as the number of full crews they currently employed.

"Ozzy really has a talent for keeping people loyal to him. We don't lose many over the winter months as he keeps the crews busy with tree trimming."

A few times Gabby interrupted her glowing recital of Ozzy's magnificence to answer her cell phone. Sometimes she spoke in Spanish and other times in English. It was obvious she was command central for Ozzy's business.

Being an efficient young lady she recommended they drop the dog off at a veterinarian she knew. The dog could get a bath and his vaccinations. It wouldn't do for Ozzy's mother to be stopped by some nosy city official asking why her dog lacked tags.

"If it's all right with you?"

Bab agreed.

After they dropped the dog off to receive both beauty and medical treatments, Bab remembered a few other errands she wanted to run. By the time they drove by a pet supply store, where Ozzy's mother wanted to buy her dog some things, the work day was nearing an end.

"As long as you don't mind if I stay in the truck?" asked Gabby. Mentally, she went through the list of things she hadn't accomplished on her to do list. "I'll use my phone's hotspot to log in with my laptop and catch up with my day."

Evelyn went through the shelves on the aisle again, reading the back of the packages. She was uncertain as to what to buy and she wanted it to be the right one.

"Open your backpack, young lady."

It was that annoying security guard that had been hovering around her since she entered the store. He always harassed the kids who visited the strip mall after school, but Evie, being black and a teenager, was his top target.

She replied belligerently, "Why?"

"Don't make it tougher on you than it's going to be," he told her. Stepping closer, he dropped one of his hands to where his taser hung at his belt. Evie sneered; did he think he was a sheriff in the wild west or something?

"I don't want to open my backpack. I know my rights."

"Then you should know this is private store property and I can make things very unpleasant for you."

"Did you find what you needed?"

The two had been so focused on their confrontation that they were surprised by the voice. Evie frowned in dismay to see Bab Dannon, her father's troublesome mother. She had seen her about a month ago when Bernard had taken her to that boring family dinner at Aunt Sarah and Uncle Arthur's house.

"Did you find it?" Bab Dannon asked her granddaughter again. The tall, white-haired white woman ignored the security guard.

To irk the guard, Evie played along with her. She held up the box containing the feeding bottle designed for puppies and kittens.

"I don't know if it will work," the girl said.

Her grandmother took the box and read the fine print without the benefit of reading spectacles.

"Look here…" the security guard began again, but Bab's confident manner made his complaint stumble to a stop.

Bab dropped Evie's box into her shopping cart next to a dog leash, collar, and some expensive dog toys. She picked up a can of kitten formula and showed it to Evie, said, "We'll need this too."

Evie grabbed a box holding the cans and put it in her grandmother's cart. Bab Dannon pushed by the guard and proceeded to the checkout, her teen granddaughter following.

Evie resisted sticking her tongue at him as she passed him.

After all she was sixteen now and far too old for something so childish.

While the cashier rang them up, Bab explained to Evie why she happened to be in the store.

"I'm actually about to return to the vet and pick up my dog."

Evie perked up and asked, "The vet? Maybe he'd see my…"

"The kittens?"

"How'd you know?"

Bab pointed to the cans of kitten formula Evie was carrying as they exited the store to the parking lot.

Evie began to explain how walking home from school, she had cut through the back of the strip mall parking lot. Hearing the kitten's weak cries, she had climbed into the garbage dumpster to rescue them. She had found three: a gray tabby, a pale orange one, and a fuzzy black one. After putting them into a cardboard box behind the store she had entered the store to find them some food.

Gabriel Morales was typing up a contract on her laptop when Bill Thompson positioned his truck to block hers from leaving. With her window down and the engine off Gabby didn't have time to react before he was leaning into her space, his fist shaking under her nose.

"You and your coward of a boss have been ignoring my calls!"

"Look, Mr. Thompson, the situation is out of my hands now. The lawyers…"

"Listen up, bitch, your man better stop sending me letters or things will go bad for you both!"

Bab's raven came over the back seat cawing and landed on the steering wheel. Gabriela had to pull back to evade the raven's flapping wings while

Thompson leapt backwards to escape as Mara seemed intent on plucking out his eyes.

In the middle of this scene, Bab loudly dropped the box of cans on the hood of Gabby's truck. The noise made them both jump.

Shooting the women dirty looks, the man climbed back into his vehicle. After slamming the truck's door, he shouted another threat at Gabriela, before revving his truck and leaving with a squeal of tires.

"What a charmer," said Bab as Gabriela climbed out of her vehicle. The woman gave a shaky laugh, obviously still upset at what had just happened.

Seeing Evelyn, Gabby said, "I didn't know you were meeting your grandmother."

"I didn't know it either," said Evie, "Who was that nasty guy?"

Gabby explained as she opened the cab doors and helped to load their purchases. Mara, the raven, hopped onto the back head rest and investigated each of the packages until Bab pulled out a package of sunflower seeds to stop his nosy behavior.

"We took a contract with the city to cut down some trees on Mr. Thompson's property to make room for new utilities. Thompson insists we did it illegally but it was on the right-of-way. He keeps writing letters to our office, the city council, and the newspaper."

"He sounded pretty scary," Evie said.

"*Las cosas se pusieron color de hormiga brava,*" Gabby

said and at Evie's confused expression, she clarified her Spanish, "things got hot there, hot as a fire ant."

The girl folded herself into the back as the two women took the front seats. Bab handed her the bag of sunflower seeds so she could feed Mara.

"*Así es el mambo,*' replied Gabby, adding for her companions, "it's just the way it is when you are dealing with someone loco."

Seeing Gabby didn't want to discuss it further, Bab turned in her seat and asked her granddaughter, "Where's those kittens?"

After collecting the box of three kittens they returned to the veterinarian's office. The front office person unlocked the door and shepherded them into a waiting room.

"You cut it pretty close. The only reason we are still here is the doc is waiting on a call from the lab."

Despite the late hour no one can resist kittens so the three orphans got a thorough health examination, were tested for parasites, and loaded down with more kitten food. Taking care of kittens turned out to be complicated and Evie got a page of instructions on how to care for them.

"You're lucky that they have their eyes open as it means they'll be easier to care for," said the vet. "I'm guessing they are about four weeks old. Just about ready to start a litter box though they'll need a little help from you to figure it all out."

All three were declared slightly dehydrated by the vet. She explained they would give them subcutaneous fluids, liquid injected under their skin. It would slowly be absorbed into their little bodies.

"Could I watch you do that?" Evie asked tentatively.

"Most don't want to see it. Are you sure?"

Evie gave a quick nod so the vet agreed.

After the girl left with the vet technician, Bab's dog was brought into the room. He immediately flopped at Bab's feet, exhausted by the horrible trial he had just been subjected to.

"¡Diantre!" exclaimed Gabby, "he looks a lot better!"

"The staff did cut out the worst of the mats but they were able to save most of his coat. I have to say we were surprised. He was incredibly patient with the whole process. You've got yourself a good dog there."

Shampoos, flea and tick medication, and an antibiotic prescription were all handed over with an explanation on how to use it.

"He has a bit of skin infection. That should clear it up but if not, bring him back in 10 days. I'd also recommend a dental sometime in the next few months."

As Bab was getting her paper work finalized, Evie re-appeared. The worn-out kittens were sound asleep in their makeshift carrier. The girl was too preoccupied talking with the vet tech to see her grandmother pull out a black credit card to pay for the charges.

They all piled back into the quad cab, a little cramped with the addition of a huge dog.

Gabby explained her plan.

"I've texted Ozzy and we agreed we'd meet up at my mom's. It's Tamale Tuesday so *mami* will be making a feast. Do you want to come with us, Evie?"

"No. I need to get home."

When they pulled up to Evie's home she insisted they stay in the car and not come to the door.

"I can carry it all," the girl replied curtly to the offers of help. Remembering her father's mother had paid for all of it and had used her white privilege to save her from a jam at the pet store, she added an abrupt thanks.

After the girl had gotten inside the house with kittens and her packages, Gabby said to Bab, "I hope you don't mind coming by my house. It will be faster than going back to the office."

"No problem," Bab said, who had already formed several opinions about Gabby Morales. One being she would be the perfect match for her middle son.

"Don't mind Evie," the woman explained. "She's touchy sometimes. A foot in both worlds and not comfortable in either."

During his time in the service, Bernard had married

a fellow soldier. Unfortunately, the next year Jasmine had gone into premature labor and died from complications when he was still deployed. Although Barney had been around as a father figure it was Evie's maternal grandmother who had truly raised her.

"Indeed," agreed Bab, knowing an aspect of her granddaughter's problems that Gabby couldn't imagine.

"Black or white? Both and neither," continued Gabby. "For me, it's always the questions about if I'm a *real* American. Of course, I am. I'm Puerto Rican!"

She took a deep breath as if to begin again but Bab quickly interrupted her.

"Tell me about that old man who was in the parking lot."

"Oh? Bill Thompson. He's loco with a tin-foil hat on his head so the government doesn't track his brain waves."

"How long has he been following you?"

Gabby gave a shocked look sideways before turning her attention back to the road.

"Following me? Where did you get that idea? I'm sure he just saw the company truck and decided to give me a scare. He's a blowhard. Oh, here's the street where my mother lives."

Seeing them drive up, Ozzy, holding a fresh sopaipilla in his hand, had just exited the house to stand on the front porch. After Gabriela lined up to park, she jumped out excitedly, hailing her boss.

"What's the news on the contract?"

"We got it," he said around a bite of his sopaipilla.

She jumped up and down, squealing and clapping her hands in joy.

"¡*Diantre!* I knew they would never be able to deny your good looks and charm!"

He laughed at her excitement, giving his mother a welcoming wave before following Gabriela into her mother's house.

Ozzy's two bedroom condo had worked well for him until a second person was added, especially someone who lived as large as his mother did.

The raven he ignored. At least the bird went outside to do his business, squeezing out a window in Bab's room she kept open for him.

The dog could have become an issue but the animal worshiped Ozzy, making it hard for the man to deny the four-legged beast anything. Within a few days, Osborne was taking the newly christened Champ with him everywhere.

"He must have been trained somewhere, mother," he told her over dinner.

His mother was eating a salad while he warmed some leftover mac-and-cheese in the microwave.

"Rarely barks. If someone is scared of him he just lays down and pretends to sleep. But when he growls at a newcomer you always know he'll turn out to be either lazy, a bully, or a thief."

He thumped the dog's ribs and Champ collapsed at his feet, in love.

"And he just adores Gabby."

"Speaking of Gabby," began Bab, her eyes wide and big like an owl, "why haven't you already proposed?"

In this Ozzy was different than his brothers: he accepted his mother for what she was. He could do this as he had inherited none of her talents and so none of the expectations.

"We started out just friends when I was working at that burger dive on the night shift. She always teased me that I'd be a business owner one day and she'd work for me. So when she finished her degree and the company was big enough, I asked her to come on board."

Unable to sit still, he got up and grabbed a beer out of the refrigerator.

"Get the grubs for me, would you?"

Ozzy collected the Styrofoam container from the fridge and handed it to his mother. She had called him earlier in the day to let him know his crossbow was ready to be picked up and when he stopped at the fish and hunting store to get it had grabbed some treats for her raven.

His mother fingered out a grub and passed it to

Mara. The raven was perched on the handle of the kitchen's three step stool, too busy reaching for his snack to pay attention to Ozzy and his love life.

"Continue with your story," Bab encouraged her son.

"This guy came along, fellow Puerto Rican, Catholic. The family loved him and they got engaged in a heartbeat."

"She doesn't wear a ring," his mother pointed out.

"Gabby caught him cheating last summer. Dropped him like a rock but he keeps coming around, begging her to take him back."

"So she's available."

"Well," Ozzy looked away, self-conscious.

"Gabby always tells the truth. If I asked her, she'd be blunt. She'd tell me straight if I had a chance. And tell me to buzz off if I didn't. Best not to rock the boat."

Gabby locked the front door and started to shut down the office. She put the petty cash and books away in the safe. The last thing on her agenda for the day was a delivery of chemicals they would need for next week. The driver was running late.

"Of course it would be the one day I agreed to meet my sister for a night out," she muttered.

Her sister always grumbled about her job, saying she worked too much. Texting Sophia that she was running late would insure yet another lecture on the matter.

Hearing the back doorbell chime, Gabby felt relieved. Maybe she could skip the lecture. In a rush, she hit the button for the dock door to open.

"About time you arrived, Toby."

She went mute seeing the gun in Bill Thompson's hand.

Cwwwwaakkkk-Cwwwwakkk said the raven, leaning forward and flaring his throat feather hackles. Bab Dannon frowned.

"Osborne, change channels to the news," she commanded her son.

Ozzy had been watching the latest sports scores, but immediately did what she asked. Seeing the ticker on the bottom of the screen, he slowly stood up, turning up the volume.

"City manager was found dead an hour ago by his wife returning home from work," the television newscaster reported. The woman was standing in front of a two story house with police cars in the background.

"There is an alert out for Bill Thompson. Police do not want you to approach him. He is considered armed and dangerous. If sighted, please call..."

"Where's Gabby?" demanded Bab.

But her son didn't answer. He grabbed the

crossbow he had left leaning against the couch and snatched his truck keys to rush out the door. His mother and dog were just as quick, right on his heels. When they hit the ground floor, they all ran for his truck.

The raven had taken the quicker route out Bab's window and he swooped down, dipping over her head.

"Scout!" she called back to her familiar.

He spread his wings to their full four-foot span, swiftly catching a draft. As the crow flies, he would make Osborne's office well before the truck, even with Bab turning every stoplight green.

Ozzy said little. Half of his mind was managing traffic, the other half was making a plan on how best to kill Bill Thompson.

Bab collected the crossbow from behind the truck seat. She knew weapons and examined it thoroughly.

"A bit different than my days in the woods."

"It's a compound crossbow."

Ozzy's words were short and clipped.

"The scope doesn't look original," observed his mother.

"A Christmas present from Barney. A night scope from his army days."

His mother picked up the crossbow's arrows and ran her fingers down their length. She spat on each metal tip and said a word that caused Ozzy to tighten his grip on the steering wheel.

"The safety is a bit noisy," his mother noted.

"I won't be using it."

As they went around to the back of the building, Ozzy cut the engine and coasted the vehicle behind a line of green dumpsters. From his position he could see the back door of the loading dock was raised. He didn't see anyone inside.

Bab leaned over and whispered, "She's alive. Mara says they are in a square room with a small window, one entrance."

Ozzy nodded understanding. There was only one area of the office that fitted that description: the break room. It was situated in the middle of the hallway that connected the back storerooms to the client area.

As he silenced his cell phone he saw several text messages from Gabriela. Ozzy replied that he was on his way and would be there within about thirty minutes. Did she want him to bring some take out?

Hopefully the message would give her some breathing room while preventing Thompson from realizing he was already here.

Very carefully, Ozzy slowly opened his truck door so as not to cause any noise. He took up a position behind the dumpster and loaded his weapon, storing the extra arrows.

Behind him a wolf bitch slipped silently out of the truck cab. She was followed in turn by the Champ. Seeing them, Ozzy narrowed his eyes.

So his mother thought to get in on this, did she?

"He's mine. Don't interfere."

Feeling the geas, the wolf gave a reluctant nod. But before he could say more she trotted away, Champ following right behind her.

"He just responded, Mr. Thompson," Gabby reassured the man with the gun. "Ozzy will be here any moment."

She hoped that Ozzy had understood the Spanish she had put in between her English texts.

If he did, the police would soon be on their way. She just needed to keep Thompson from killing her before they arrived.

After Gabriela had been surprised at the door, Thompson had roughly shoved her ahead of him, forcing her down the hallway. The blood on his clothes had shocked her to silence and she was quick to comply with his demands.

He had brought her to the office breakroom with only one doorway and a window small and high on the wall. Through the frosted glass, she could see a silhouette of a black bird, too big to be a pigeon, strutting about on the ledge.

From his rants it seemed the only reason she was still alive was because he wanted her to draw Ozzy to the office. He planned on shooting Gabby in front of her boyfriend.

With his pacing and gun waving she wondered if he was on drugs. A cop acquaintance had once told her you couldn't predict someone's behavior if they were *arrebatao,* causing her to worry more.

"Call him again you wetback bitch," Thompson said, kicking one of the chairs against the wall. "This time put it on speaker phone."

Her fingers shaking, Gabby touched the contact number in her phone for Ozzy. She hoped he would respond, but at the same time wished he wouldn't.

Her call went to voice mail. She left a message, meeting Thompson's wild eyes the entire time she spoke.

"Ozzy when are you going to get here? Can you give me a call back?"

When Gabriela finished, she told Thompson that Ozzy never answered his phone while driving. While that wasn't strictly true she hoped Ozzy's non-response meant he was already on his way with the police.

Before Thompson could quarrel with her again, a noise started down the hall that shocked them both to stillness.

It was the hollow echoing sound of a wild beast.

It wasn't the type of sound you'd hear from a television set or a phone. It was raw, real, and in the building.

The wolf's howling summoned a primal response of deep fear from Gabriela. It made the hair on the woman's neck prickle; goosebumps formed down her forearms. Thompson made her afraid but he was a known, even predictable threat. This was out-of-place, unexpected, and more frightening because of it.

Even in his mental state, Bill Thompson was also affected by the bizarreness of the sound.

"What the hel-" the man began but Thompson stopped talking when the wolf came through the doorway.

Unmistakably, a wolf.

Much bigger than Champ.

In coloring, she was much like a domesticated Husky but her coarse thick coat had a pronounced mane. The gray-white shades had undertones of rust. But it was her eyes - the orange alien and inhuman eyes that kept them both paralyzed.

Under their stunned gaze, she dropped and crawled forward on her belly. The wolf rolled onto her side like a puppy seeking a belly rub.

Thompson raised his gun to shoot when two things happened at once: behind him Gabby seized the glass coffee pot sitting on the kitchen counter and slammed it against the back of the man's head; and Osborne stepped into the doorway in a crouch, and shot off a bolt from his crossbow.

Surprised, Thompson's finger instinctively squeezed the trigger and the gun went off twice while he staggered sideways. Champ emerged from behind his owner and body-slammed Thompson to the floor, causing him to drop the gun. The dog's fierce growling, the arrow in his shoulder, and the loss of his handgun kept Thompson from rising.

For once Osborne forgot to be quiet and stoic. He was holding the woman he loved and she was in his arms, hugging him back just as fiercely.

"Gabby! Are you all right? Did he hurt you? I'll kill him…"

"Ozzy, Ozzy," was all she kept saying.

"It's going to be all right," he said, squeezing her fiercely.

At his words Gabby burst into tears.

When the police and ambulance arrived, Ozzy could have cared less about Bill Thompson getting treated for an arrow stuck in his shoulder. He told everyone it was really Gabriela who should be wrapped up in a blanket and taken to the hospital for an immediate medical exam.

"There's no need," she protested but Ozzy insisted.

"People can die from a shock like this," her

protector said. Persuaded by Ozzy, they left in the second ambulance.

The sensational nature of the confrontation with Bill Thompson called for a quick response from the hospital. Instead of waiting in a crowded emergency room area, Gabby found herself being whisked away in a wheelchair to a private room.

Looking down into the parking lot from the hospital window, Barney observed the quantity of media news vans setting up outside. He told her, "You're the heroine of the hour."

"Oh no," Gabby protested, "Ozzy was the one with the cojones to take him on."

Looking down at her with pride, Ozzy said, "If you hadn't hit him with that coffee pot my arrow would have struck him square in the chest."

She pressed Osborne's hand and kissed it. On the opposite side of the bed sat her mother, her eyes red from crying, holding Gabby's other hand.

The families had met up at the hospital, and after the excited explanations, Bab Dannon had removed Evie and Logan to the cafeteria for a round of snacks.

When Gabby started to look tired, the oldest and youngest brothers also made their excuses to leave. Besides it looked like Gabby and Ozzy had a lot to say to each other.

Walking down the hospital corridor to the elevator,

Arthur asked Barney, "You don't think mother had anything to do with this Thompson guy going crazy do you?"

Barney gave his brother's comment serious consideration before replying slowly, "No. From what Ozzy described it seems this guy was a threat long before she came on the scene. They just didn't realize how seriously off the rails he was."

Arthur grunted and pushed the button for the elevator. While they waited, Barney asked after his wife.

"I haven't seen either of you since the fallout with mother. How is Sarah doing?"

"She's okay."

"Really?" Barney's eyebrows were skeptical. When Artie squirmed under his gaze he knew his instinct had been right. His brother was hiding something.

The elevator doors opened, and seeing the passengers it carried, Barney silently promised himself he'd remember to ask more questions next time they were private.

Logan had been full of questions, wanting to know how Mara and Champ had helped with the rescue. Evelyn was more reticent. Her eyes roamed about as if avoiding her grandmother's and she nervously picked at her fingernails.

"How are the kittens doing?"

Evie startled at being addressed directly by Bab; clearly her attention had not been with the group. Her polite reply of "fine" was interrupted by Logan's, "You have kittens? I wish I had one."

"Good, because I have three and I'm looking for homes."

"I don't know if my mom…"

"Just like I thought," the girl snapped back at him. "No help as usual, Logan."

Logan was crushed, not only at not having a kitten, but at Evie's curt manner.

Before kittens could be discussed further, Barney and Arthur arrived. Logan's dad put a hand on his son's shoulder and said it was time to go. The two were almost through the automatic doors when the boy ran back to his grandmother.

He whispered in Bab's ear, "Mom thinks she's dead. She needs your help," before racing back to his father.

Within the week, Gabriela and Osborne announced their engagement. The couple would be taking a week off from work to fly with her mother back to Puerto Rico for a visit. This would give Ozzy a chance to meet Gabby's extended family, all properly chaperoned by her mother, while the media excitement about the Thompson affair quieted down.

While they were gone, Bab would stay at his condo looking after Champ, who Ozzy now considered irrevocably his dog.

Bernard dreamed.

He was sitting in a MRAP, his spine being jolted like a jackhammer because of the crappy level of comfort the army transport vehicle gave. His teeth slammed together and with the heat and his dry lips, he knew where he was. Back in Iraq.

"Fun ride isn't it?" joked the black woman sitting next to him.

She had a thousand watt smile and big eyes with the curliest lashes he had ever seen. It bothered him that he couldn't remember who she was.

He *should* have known who she was.

"We need your magic to put everything right."

"I don't do that any more."

As dreams do, this one shifted without warning but in a way that seemed perfectly rational. He was in Arthur's house, standing in his brother's kitchen. Barney was still wearing his OCP's, helmet, and his M16 hung on his shoulder.

He was armed for combat.

As he walked through the rooms on the first floor all was quiet, no appliances hummed, no voices were heard inside or out. Barney felt that familiar warning chill on the back of his neck.

Instinctively, he brought his weapon down and

prepped it; his hands automatically going through the familiar motions.

He called out for Artie, Logan, and even Sarah. No one answered him. He was about to go up to the second floor when he saw his sister-in-law at the top of the staircase.

"They are all dead. We are all dead," she said.

Sarah held out her hands to him, right before all her skin and flesh melted off and her bones tumbled down the steps.

Barney woke up drenched in his own sweat, his heartbeat revving like a race car.

It had been years since he had such a dream. After his wife died he had deliberately put his talent for premonition, the lucky guess, and his abilities to help the dying, all away in a mental box. Locked it all up and thrown it down into a deep abyss of forgetting.

If his talent couldn't help Jasmine, he didn't need it.

He fixed some coffee. He made it black, wanting the bitter taste to wipe out that metallic taste coating his tongue. Sipping the beverage he looked at the framed photo of his wife that he kept hanging on the wall.

"C'mon, Jazzy, you know I'd never forget you."

She didn't answer, but even dead, she could get him to do whatever she wanted.

Barney called into work for the day off. They weren't happy about it but they could suck it. He hadn't called in sick since he started working there five years ago so about time he did. They were getting a bit too complacent about him being the one to cover everyone else's shift.

After a shower, he sorted through the pile of clothes on the floor and found the cleanest pair of jeans.

Barney took off on his bike and went to have a talk with his mother.

"If you would just open your closed mind, perhaps you'd find something of worth there."

Barney found Bab Dannon standing on the sidewalk, barefoot, wearing a MuMu with a psychedelic print of flowers, and arguing with a thin, older man who wore glasses.

His mother's long white hair was out of its braid, messed up in the back as if she had just rolled out of bed. When Barney approached he smelled the Ylang Ylang and sandalwood so knew his mother had been up to what she called her love training.

"I just don't like different men tramping in here day and night. It looks shady."

"Are you accusing me of running a brothel?" demanded Bab, hands on her hips. "For your information Mr. Nosy I don't charge money for my

Tantric lessons."

"The neighborhood association is going to hear about this," the neighbor warned her. Seeing Barney and taking in his size, he quickly walked away while Bab shouted after him, "You do that!"

She invited her youngest son inside.

"I don't want to disturb you and your guests, mom."

"Oh they've already left."

Barney followed, closing the door behind him. His brother's condo was a townhouse, the first floor a small living room, kitchen, and powder room. The upstairs had two bedrooms, one a loft, and a full bath.

He had a lifetime to know how his mother lived so he wasn't surprised, like Logan had been, by the transformation of Ozzy's tidy bachelor-pad all in neutrals and chrome to one of tie-dye hedonism.

She poured them some orange juice and handed him a tumbler. He sipped it cautiously, knowing from experience the strange concoctions his mother could assemble.

"Fresh squeezed," his mother reassured him. With her back to him, she jammed some thick bagel slices into the toaster.

"I had a dream this morning."

"Dreams are only dreams. They don't hold much meaning nowadays."

"It was one of *those* dreams," he said, but Barney

knew she understood his meaning the first time. Bab ignored him, busy using a fork to pry out a well-toasted bagel slice from the machine.

"Jazzy was in it. She said I needed to use my magic."

"Maybe you'll listen to her when you haven't listened to the rest of us. You have a daughter, you know. Maybe spend some time being a dad."

"What does Evie have to do with this?" Barney replied, irked. Where did his mother get off advising him on how to parent?

"I guess you didn't know she has a Gift. Some dad you are."

At his mother's words, Barney felt the floor underneath him drop. He put his hands on the counter to steady himself.

"No - can you take it away? Remove it? I don't want Evie to…"

"Suffer like you did? Life is suffering, kiddo, and you need to grow up."

Having eaten her bagel in a few neat bites, Bab leaned a hip against the kitchen counter. She crossed her arms, thrusting her chin forward in a stubborn posture Arthur knew all too well.

"I know you blame yourself for Jasmine's death but things happen. The Wheel of Fortune spins and sometimes it's a Wheel of Catherine that crushes us instead."

"I should have been there! I could have saved her!"

"Nope. You couldn't. I don't know why you think you're some kind of god who decides such things but you aren't."

"I saved comrades in Iraq," Barney said, resisting her logic. "I brought them back from death. I KNOW I did."

"Nope again kiddo. Whoever you helped wanted to come back. All you did was put a bridge in place to help them return. But sometimes willpower and desire isn't enough. If you want to blame anyone, blame that jackass of a doctor who kept denying your wife was in pain."

"What would you know of it?"

"Because I was there when Jazzy died. I held her hand. By the time I reached her, Barney, she had no choice about staying."

He hadn't known she was there at Evie's birth. When Barney had arrived weeks after Jazzy's death, no one had thought to tell him. He covered his face with his hands and Bab gave him a pat on the back, rocking him gently against her. He was her youngest, most favorite, and most talented child.

"Can we flush that guilt right down the toilet with the other shit? For over a decade you've used used it to block your Gift and right now it's needed. Sarah needs you back in the game."

"Sarah? Sarah was in that dream too," Barney

remembered, rubbing his forehead.

"Logan told me she thinks she's dead."

"WHAT?" Barney who had seen and heard some pretty crazy things in his life thought this was probably the craziest. It was all well and good to have a weird dream but not for it to become a summer horror movie come to life.

"She's not a zombie. Get real, Barney," Bab said seeing Barney's expression. "But she did go through a near-death experience and is probably just confused. I think we should go see her. Arthur should be at work today since it's Monday."

"I don't know, mom. Going behind Artie's back? That doesn't sound like a good idea."

"Oh, so that dream makes you think we can wait? That everything is okay?"

"Definitely *not* okay," Barney said, grimacing, the aftertaste of prophecy in his mouth reminding him.

Evie woke up with a familiar feeling that haunted her all day. She didn't like the uneasy vibe she'd get knowing something was about to go wrong.

Sometimes it would be something as minor as a test score or a flat tire on her grandmother's car. Once it predicted a public humiliation at school when her backpack zipper broke, spilling her schoolbooks and sketches, right in front of the popular clique.

She had been teased about her wolf drawings for

the entire school year.

From experience though Evelyn knew there was nothing to be done except to ride it out and stay home.

That should be easy as she was off from school since the teachers were having a professional day. Evie thought it a lucky break because she wanted to cram for a Tuesday test.

Evie's concentration was interrupted after lunch by the doorbell. She was surprised to see her cousin Logan at the door. Peering through the screen door, she demanded, "What are you doing here?"

"I came to see the kittens. I want one."

"Your mom will never let you have a pet."

"I talked to her. She told me I could."

Evie scoffed but opened the door. Logan gave an eloquent description of the conversation he had with his mother that was so elaborate a lie that Evelyn was impressed despite herself.

She went and collected the kittens from her room, bringing them and a few cat toys to the living room. She was down to two since a friend of her grandmother's, a really good-looking firefighter guy, had dropped by to pick up the orange one.

"Let me hold one," said Logan excitedly.

Evie handed the tabby striped kitten over before settling down, cross-legged, on the floor with her own black kitten.

She explained what they liked and didn't, what they ate, how to clean their litter box, and how to pet them. She let him know only the tabby was still available. She was keeping the black kitten.

"That's okay," said Logan. "I want this one anyway. She's special."

He was lying on his stomach while the gray tabby with the white legs and stomach climbed over his back, batting at his hair. Like only children can do, Logan felt a pure unadulterated love for the little creature and vowed nothing would ever separate him from her. He'd convince his mother somehow to let him keep her.

"It's a deal but if your mom backs out of it, she comes right back to me," Evie warned. "I won't have you re-gifting her to someone I don't know."

Logan had taken the bus cross-town so Evelyn agreed to help her cousin bring the kitten home. Besides she wanted to see how her Aunt Sarah was going to react for despite Logan's reassurances, Evie highly suspected she was going to return with the kitten.

She got a grocery bag to put in some clean litter, another bag for cat food, and a few toys.

Evie had been given a cardboard travel box at the vet's office. It would do for transporting Tabatha, the newly christened kitty, to Logan's house but the pet carrier would be too obvious to take on the public bus.

"What we need is something to conceal the carrier so the bus driver will let us on," explained Evie.

Logan suggested they use a school backpack instead.

"I'll just make sure I keep the top zipper open just enough so she can breathe," Logan showed Evie.

Their plans made, the three set off to Logan's house.

Sarah didn't wonder why two strangers were in her house.

After all she was dead.

Maybe Arthur had put the house up for sale since she drowned?

"Why doesn't she recognize us?" asked the man. He had sandy brown hair and a friendly face with hazel eyes. He'd look more pleasant if he wasn't frowning.

The older woman accompanying him frightened Sarah, but it was a remote, faraway feeling that didn't quite touch her.

However, it wasn't as easy to ignore people, even when you were dead. Especially when they invaded your house and pinched your arm.

Bab Dannon frowned as she watched her daughter-in-law sitting in the chair. She hadn't seen her for a couple of months and the woman was noticeably thinner. Her hair was unkempt and she wore no make-up. Even her clothes seemed a haphazard collection as if it had been Artie who had picked out them out instead of his wife.

"We've got a problem." Bab's statement earned her an eye roll from Barney who replied, "Duh."

His mother disregarded his sarcasm and bent down so her eyes were at the level of Sarah's. Bab leaned over, mere inches away, but Sarah's face remained blank and unresponsive.

Standing up, Bab put her hand to her chin, considering the problem that was her daughter-in-law.

"The essential part is missing. The personality, the capacity to feel emotions. The soul of who she is."

"Gone? Gone where?"

"Where do you think?" Bab replied, exasperated. "Why do you think you had that dream, Bernard? What is your talent? Walking the bridge between the worlds. You'll have to go and retrieve her soul and bring it back."

"Why me? You're the one who caused all this!" Barney sputtered. Sarah presented a very big problem that he felt incapable of solving.

"That ritual back in March, the drowning in the pool - all of it is *your* fault. mom. Besides, you're far more powerful than I am."

"I'm not here to do your job for you, kiddo. We've already had that discussion. Time for you to grow up and do what you were born to do."

The two continued to bicker, oblivious to the two children who had entered the house. Evie and Logan, upon hearing voices, had followed the sound to discover their owners.

As the two adults argued, their increasing temper, as well as the topic of what they were discussing, made the two children exchange glances.

"Can you help my mom?"

Bab and Barney turned as one to see the boy holding a squirming ball of fur that was trying to climb up his shoulder. Evie was loaded down with a big backpack and a couple of sacks.

"We are both here to help your mother, kiddo," said his grandmother, gesturing for him to come towards her. "But I think you, Logan, could help her the most."

Turning to Barney she clarified.

"Take Logan with you. Sarah's love for her child will be a powerful magnet to draw her to you."

"I'm not taking a boy with me. It's perilous enough," began Bernard but was interrupted by his nephew who stated firmly, "I'm going."

Before they could argue further, Evie said in a voice so odd, so strange, that even Sarah (who couldn't be bothered because she was dead) turned to stare at her.

"Without him your journey's wandering will have no end."

"See," said Bab, smugly, "a bard is always useful on

jobs like this."

Logan had heard his dad on the phone making medical appointments for his mother. Eavesdropping, Logan had heard the word *Cotard*. After reading about the Walking Corpse Syndrome on the Internet it explained why his mother wanted to visit the cemetery. But it did not reassure him she would be okay without help.

"So what do I do?" Logan asked.

He was nervous but ready to get started. Even now the boy could see that his mother's mind had wandered away again.

"Okay Logan. Let me try to explain what we are going to do. There's another land where we go to when we die," Barney started but was shut down by his daughter.

"Cut the BS dad. Logan's in Gifted and Talented at a private school. He doesn't need you to talk to him like he's five."

Evie took over the explanation and told Logan the bald facts.

"Look, Logan, your mom had a near death experience thanks to Granny's hippie party. Because her body died for a moment, she's confused about where she should be. My dad can go talk to her soul and convince it to return. That's what he does - or used to do."

If Barney felt uncomfortable before he felt doubly embarrassed now. He hadn't known Evie was aware of his past.

"Yeah, I know dad. Mom left journals behind and grandma boxed up all her stuff for me." Evie crossed her arms, her tone belligerent. "Maybe if you'd stop thinking I'm a baby we could talk about things like bringing back the dead."

"I couldn't save your mother," Barney told her, his voice breaking. Evelyn nodded at his words but seeing all the emotions she was trying to suppress her father wrapped his daughter into his arms. It took a few moments but she hugged him back just as fiercely.

"I know you would have saved her if you could," she mumbled into his chest. "If you can help Aunt Sarah, you need to try."

Most of Bab Dannon's belongings had been left in the guest house as there simply wasn't enough room at Osborne's apartment for her collection. The five of them tramped through the backyard, with Logan firmly holding onto his mother's hand or she would not have come with them.

From somewhere, Bab's raven, Mara, had appeared. He flew through the open French doors and settled himself up high on one of the open exposed beams. From his summit he could see them all as they set up for the ritual.

Bab placed Sarah in a chair as she directed the others on where to find incense, matches, and candles. Using chalk that Evie had given her, Bab started drawing a pattern on the tile floor around Sarah.

Logan had watched a lot of television shows and played many video games. He felt he was hip to what granny was attempting.

"I thought you'd do a pentagram. What are those lines?"

"These lines make ancient words - but they also have other powers. Like when a phrase means something more than the words translate. *Avaler des couleuvres.*"

Logan translated the French easily.

"Swallow grass snakes? That doesn't make sense."

"Exactly! It means more than its translation. Ask Celine to explain it," said Bab, referring to the French girl that Logan was tutoring in English.

"The fact is that symbols and words gain power, and mean different things than originally intended, the longer people use and believe in them."

"And the incense? And candles?"

"The incense harnesses the power of the plants and sends a message to the heavens. We also inhale those properties. Candles? Candles I just find pretty."

Wiping her hands free of chalk dust she put Logan between his mother and Bernard.

"No matter what happens," Bab warned Logan,

"do not let go of your Uncle Barney's hand."

Barney thought he might have trouble entering the proper state of meditation. He worried he'd struggle with his Gift since it had been so long but it opened to him as easily as an unlocked door.

He walked across the bridge holding Logan's hand.

"Why are we at the mall?" asked his nephew, looking around curiously.

"The landscape is created by Sarah, your mom's, mind," explained Barney.

And yes, the place was spooky as hell. An image of an apocalyptic zombie world but Barney didn't tell the kid that.

The mall was devoid of people and being made from fragments of Sarah's memory wasn't accurate or even all in focus. The dream-scape had an intangible depth so where you looked the edges were sharp but anything on the fringe lacked definition.

"Where's my mom?"

"Call her."

The boy's voice hadn't changed yet, but he could make it loud.

"Barney what are you doing here? Logan?"

When Sarah appeared Logan threw himself against her so hard she rocked back on her high heels.

"I came to the mall to get something but I can't remember what it was," she said, giving Logan back his hug. "Was it to pick you up, Logan? Or was it to get some shirts for your dad?"

Barney wasn't listening to Logan's reunion as he was having his own. He rubbed his eyes and when he opened them again, his dead wife, Jasmine, was still standing in front of him. He was afraid to touch her because in the ephemeral, shadows looked real and reality was only mist.

"Hey Baby Bear," she greeted him with her pet name.

His heart remembered its pain, aching not only for the loss of her, but for all those he had known, who he had worked and soldiered beside. Loss of direction, loss of hope, loss of belief.

Any desire to return to the living faded away.

Jazzy came so close he could smell her perfume, the scent almost forgotten. She tapped her forefinger on his chest, hitting the metal of the two dog tags he always kept on a chain around his neck.

He could feel a heat, an aching warmth, but also healing.

He wasn't as broken as he had been.

She gave him a kiss on the cheek.

"Give this to babygirl when you see her again."

When Arthur arrived home and discovered what his mother was doing, he turned into a bear.

If he was imposing as a man, as a bear he was terrifying. His bulk was massive, bigger than Bab's Smart car, and his powerful arms ended in paws larger than Evie's head. The teenager covered her mouth but the scream couldn't emerge from her frozen throat.

"Just calm down Arthur," his mother said soothingly causing her son to roar.

"I want my wife and son here now!" He shook his head back and forth, opening his jaws with a snarl. "Badb Catha bring them back!"

"I'm constrained," the goddess said, narrowing her eyes at Arthur. "I cannot interfere with their destinies."

In his rage, Arthur the bear rose to his full imposing height, his wide head touching the ceiling. "Was it destiny that brought you here? Upended our lives? Put my loved ones in danger?"

"Perhaps," Badb said, crossing her arms, but refusing to budge or divulge. "Logan must come to his Gift."

"You do not make decisions for *my* family!"

The roaring made Evelyn cover her ears. She cowered down behind her father.

Despite all the noise Barney and Logan did not awake from their trance while Sarah only gave a vaguely curious glance at her husband.

Mara, who had been waiting for a dramatic point to make his entrance, spoke.

"It is permitted that those on the journey can have a guide. I like the bard and shall go."

Before he could be stopped and with theatrical flare, he was engulfed in a fireball; the flames replaced by a dense puff of black smoke. As he vanished, a lone iridescent black feather drifted down to land in Evelyn's lap.

"You seem to be in a bit of a pickle, bard."

Logan felt only relief with the appearance of his granny's raven. The two adults had both failed him. Barney said he couldn't remember the path back and his mother was crying.

Mara would help.

"Can you show us the way home?"

"The way home is in your heart. I cannot teach you what your heart knows."

"Don't talk in riddles," retorted the boy who was starting to feel nervous and uncertain again. Like his mother, when feeling unpleasant emotions he replaced it with those he found more acceptable, such as irritation.

"It is only a riddle because you don't know the answer," Mara said. "Your uncle's heart has betrayed him. He yearns for things he cannot have so his path is gone."

"I don't understand."

"It is good that you do not. The young have an

intensity for life because they lack experience; the old gain wisdom from experience, but they sometimes lack a surety of belief."

The raven cocked his head as he did an odd hop-skip walk to come closer to where Logan stood, holding the hands of his mother and uncle.

"Do you want that kitten? Badb was telling Evie she has another friend who'd take it."

"What?" cried Logan, "That isn't fair! She promised Tabatha to me!"

"You better tell her quick because I hear her giving it away even now."

And in a snap, Logan brought them all back across the bridge between the worlds. The boy opened his eyes to see the comfortable familiarity of home. He shot Evie a look of betrayal.

His mother's eyes fluttered and she looked around with natural confusion.

"Artie why are you a bear? And what happened to my blue sofa cushions?"

Badb was given her marching papers. Both sons wanted her gone.

Logan was allowed a brief and supervised goodbye. On the other hand, Evie felt old enough to make up her own mind so she was helping her grandmother pack.

"I don't understand how all of this will fit into your

car?"

"Don't you watch the BBC? Inner and outer size is relative. What I need will fit and what doesn't you can have or give away."

"Where's Mara?" Evie hadn't seen the raven since he had left her a feather.

"Oh he's about," said Badb, vaguely waving her hand. "He likes to go off and have his own adventures. He'll return when he's ready."

Evelyn decided not to ask how the bird would know were Badb was; maybe he was part homing pigeon. Overall, she didn't know what to make of all the events of the previous day.

She also didn't think she'd get any explanation.

Uncle Arthur (returned to human form) and Aunt Sarah (returned from the dead) had taken Logan (and kitten) back to the main house. Evie figured between Logan's sweet talk and all the crap his parents had gone through, her cousin would be able to keep Tabatha as a consolation prize.

For how could his parents deny him a kitten when he was the hero of the hour?

Her father had given Evelyn her mother's dog tag. Seeing the name had made Evie cry but not too much as she was practically grown up. Bernard gave her a rough hug and promised he'd set time aside later for them to talk.

Her grandmother though did have a few bits of advice before she left.

"Things are going to get complicated for you, kiddo. Lean on your dad. Get him to explain things. He knows you'll need help but he'll need a nudge or two to remember to give it."

"My life is complicated enough. I don't think I need more thank you very much," said Evie.

She rolled up another batik print and stuffed it through the back window of Badb's car. Everything inside seemed to move to allow room for it just as Badb said.

"Oh honey, you don't know anything about complications," laughed her grandmother, putting on her sunglasses. "Wait until you fall in love."

"That isn't a prophecy is it?" Evie asked suspiciously.

"We all fall in love. I don't need my powers to tell me that," Badb settled a big straw hat down on her head and climbed into the driver's seat of her tiny car.

"I will say the test on Tuesday is going to be postponed until Thursday. Your teacher went to a bachelorette party and she won't be feeling up to teaching high schoolers."

"Oh, thanks!"

"I've muted your powers so you can grow up. After all you've college to get through."

"No college for me. No money."

Granny cackled.

"Oh honey, you'll be going to college and it's going to be a blast. But I can't stop what's going to happen to you when you turn thirty."

"What? Wait. What's going to happen when I turn thirty?"

"Toodaloo!" Badb shouted, waving one hand out the window, honking her horn with the other as she drove away.

After Evie waved her grandmother goodbye she decided she better go and give Logan more advice about how to care for Tabatha before her father came to collect her.

Thirty was a lifetime away. Almost double the age she was now. She'd think about it later.

The Morrighan

An Irish Goddess, the Morrighan, The Great
Queen, Queen of the Dead, Queen of Phantoms, is
affiliated with land rule, sovereignty and queenship.

In Celtic tales, she used sorcery, Druidic magic, and
shapeshifting to crow, raven, cow, wolf, and eel, to
give aid. She can appear as either an old or young
woman, and is tied to fertility. In some tales she often
mates with the chosen war-leader.

In *Granny Starseed*, I chose to use her lesser well-
known name - Badb Catha or the Battle Crow. This
aspect is aligned with the otherworldly powers of
battle and battle sorcery, warriors and bloodshed, as
well as prophecy and poetry.

Granny Starseed Spanish

Gabby uses several expressions from Puerto Rico.

Hermano - brother

Mami - mother

Baile, botella y baraja - Translates to "Dance, Bottle, and Cards." Alludes to premeditated plans to keep someone entertained while others (usually, the government) does their job or duties. A phrase used by historians to describe the government of Miguel de la Torre (1822-1837).

Las cosas se pusieron color de hormiga brava - things are the color of the fire ant (and if you've ever been been involved with fire ants you know exactly what this phrase means - hot!).

Así es el mambo - That's how you dance the Mambo or that is just the way it happens, the nature of the beast.

Loco - crazy

¡Diantre! - Wow

Arrebatao - on drugs

cojones - balls, testicles

Thank you to Gutenberg for serving as a reference.

Never Date a Siren

College Life: Friends, Finals, and the Fae trying to kill you.

A YA contemporary fantasy world where beings from the Perilous Realm make university life for humans precarious.

Brigit, a fae runaway, didn't plan on getting a human roommate. Or that she would be placed under a fairy debt. Will the dryad be able to save Logan from a siren's love spell or fail the semester?

Read on for a preview of this exciting new story —

Never Date a Siren, Chapter One

Brigit lost her apartment a week after midterms in the spring semester. It didn't help her grades or her mood.

"Look on the bright side," said Celia, "at least you won't have to deal with Sam's messes anymore."

"I'll be glad not to live with a pig, but he had no right to throw me out." At her angry statement, Celia reminded Brigit of her warning about getting involved with the temperamental Sam in the first place.

"I told you when you refused to sign that lease you'd have no recourse if things went poorly. And with Sam, they were bound to go poorly."

Brigit didn't tell Celia the reason she hadn't signed the lease was it required a background check. As it was, the freshman had already lied about several things on the college application she had submitted last fall to the Leopold Otto University in Geheimetür.

Leopold Otto was the only higher learning institution in the human lands even willing to admit the troublesome fae to their program. Indeed, the country of Bewachterberg was friendly to her kind because of the Treaty of Sigismund. But Brigit, with the suspicious and skeptical traits native to the fae, knew welcomes could be withdrawn.

Not willing to discuss the apartment lease any further, Brigit dipped a spoon into some of the cheesy Spätzle from Celia's plate and ate it while looking about the hall. The two students were seated in the university's main cafeteria, a building over 400 years old which once had been the infirmary of the original monastery building complex. Brigit loved the soaring ceilings, the exposed ancient wooden beams, and the floor-to-ceiling coffered wall paneling.

The aged wood gave the dryad pleasant shivers.

"You'll just have to find another roommate," scolded Celia. "Before you ask, you can't sleep on my couch. I already have three squatting in a two-bed apartment with only one bathroom. As it is I'm about ready to kick out Katey's free-loading boyfriend."

Brigit sighed and ran a hand over her forehead, causing tight black curls to briefly pull back from her face, revealing deep brown, almost black eyes. Like many of the fae, she was thin. It gave her a deceptive appearance of frailty; in reality, she was twice as strong as a human of the same outward appearance.

"I can't sleep in the library one more night with those ghosts. I guess after you die, you give up any sort of decency."

Celia pursed her lips, leaning back into her chair, as she considered Brigit's problem. She was a curvy woman with long, curly chestnut hair, a friendly countenance that held sea-green-blue eyes, and a mild smile.

The two fae had met during the last semester and had bonded over several things: they were both of the fae Sept, or clan, of naturals as Brigit was a dryad and Celia a naiad, and they had despised the biology professor teaching the class they shared.

The dining tables in the hall were filling up with students. Celia's eyes found a target, and she leaned over to tell Brigit, "What about that guy? Stop. Don't look yet. Yeah, he's seated now."

The nursing student dropped a napkin off the side of the table and gave an expressive sideways glance to where it fell to her friend. Brigit pushed her seat back and bent to pick it up, taking a casual look under her arm in the direction where her companion had indicated.

A male human with dark hair was seated two tables over by himself. He was looking through a textbook while ignoring the Gulasch before him.

"Him? What about him?"

"I hear he has a two-bed apartment. Very nice. One of those new downtown lofts. Roomy. I bet it has lots of windows, unlike Sam's cave dwelling."

"How would you know about it? Been inside?"

"He visited the dispensary during my rotation, and we chatted. He's here as an exchange student. The university is so desperate for money they let him bend the rules and room off-campus. The grapevine says he's from a stinking rich American family, so I bet there's no week's worth of instant noodles in his pantry cabinet."

"But he's a human, Ceel," protested Brigit. Last fall was the first time she had been around humans since leaving the Perilous Realm. They still disconcerted her; their energy fields weren't exactly unpleasant, just strange. Brigit had not struck up any relationships with them yet and wasn't sure she would.

"It'd be weird. I've never shared with a human before."

"At least go look it over. Never hurts to know

what's out there."

***

The student finally got off the bus, and Brigit watched him pass her window, seeing his face in profile before the bus pulled forward again. She waited for two more stops before hopping off herself. Circling the block, she came across the street to observe him mounting steps into a flat-faced, red brick building. While it was new, it mimicked the older construction on either side of it.

Brigit lightly touched the flowers and trees in the planters on the sidewalk. She greeted the plants as she edged herself closer to where the young man had entered.

"Beetle dung, a keypad," the dryad muttered under her breath as she saw her first real obstacle. "What do I do now?"

Generally, the fae weren't compatible with technology, though most managed to exist with it. However, Brigit's problem with communication tech was so significant the university had given her a disability waiver. Instead of a computer, she pounded out her class papers on an antique typewriter in the basement of the library. Lacking a mobile phone in the human lands was a big inconvenience, but it was a fact that cell phone batteries died if she touched them.

Brigit saw someone inside come to the front glass door, so she quickly skipped up the steps and grabbed the door before the guy exiting could shut it. Not looking back, Brigit made her way to the bank of elevators and made a show of pushing an "up" button.

By the time the elevator doors opened, the resident was no longer in view. Ignoring the elevator's open doors, she walked over to the end of the lobby. Standing in front of a row of mailboxes she dug into a pocket on her backpack.

She retrieved a pendulum with a stone carved from moss agate held on a silver chain. She let the stone warm up in her palm while she told it what was needed. Feeling its readiness to assist her, Brigit held the pendulum up to the row of numbers, moving it slowly in front of the mailboxes one at a time.

She had a bit of *Finder* in her fae bloodline, and the pendulum didn't fail her. It swayed harder in front of one particular box, indicating the apartment she wanted was on the third floor.

Knowing how lazy humans were, and disliking technology herself, the fae took the stairs to lessen the possibility of meeting someone. At each landing were small, narrow windows providing a bit of light and a potted plant squeezed into the corner. Brigit took a moment to give each plant a spark of her dryad energy. In her experience, indoor plants could always use a bit extra to keep them well.

She found apartment 305 at the end of the hall. In front of the door was a coco fiber welcome mat and since no one was in view, she knelt, and asked it, "Would you like to help me?"

I welcome people! Welcome. Hi! How are you?

It had a coarse, grating kind of voice in her head. Brigit's abilities let her communicate with organic material, whether it was living or not. She stroked the fibers with her fingers and palm, causing it to shiver under her hand.

"I need inside."

Help you! I'm a Helper! Wipe feet!

The palm situated at the dead-end of the hallway, just a few steps away, interrupted their conversation with a slight furry cough.

The man will leave in a moment with his laundry basket. I've heard the laundry is in the basement. I've never been there personally.

"Thanks."

Brigit formulated a quick plan, and after giving them instructions, she slipped back down the hall to the stairs. There she cracked the door slightly and took a seat on the top step in the stairwell. The freshman spent the time reading and highlighting a textbook to prepare for her chemistry test.

Engrossed in her work, Brigit missed the click of

the apartment door. Luckily, the palm plant called out to her in its sonorous voice: *There he goes on schedule. I'm never wrong about my people.*

Peering through the slit between door and frame, she saw the human was waiting at the elevator, holding a basket of clothes against his hip. He had changed to a more casual outfit, now wearing a dark blue t-shirt and shorts. He seemed preoccupied as he at first didn't respond to the elevator ding. Only when the elevator doors started to close did he put out his hand to stop their motion and finally entered the lift.

Seeing him gone, Brigit crept out into the hallway and hustled back to his apartment door.

Welcome! Come in! Greetings!

Like she had requested, the doormat had edged itself over the threshold, a corner of it preventing the front door from closing and thus stopping the lock from engaging.

"What a good welcoming mat you are."

The ebook is FREE at your favorite online bookseller. Visit www.byrdnash.com/ndas for more details!

Author Notes

Author Notes

With the flurry of trying to write and get a book ready to press, there are so many I wish to thank in addition to my dedications.

Beta readers for *Wicked Wolves* included some long-time social media followers: Jessica F., Cori Z., Liz R., Astrid M., and Sara G. All provided invaluable feedback as the stories developed, helping me to improve them from their rough drafts. My editor and Kate H. kept me on my toes.

Thank you for reading my collection of fantasy fairytales. I'm so glad you took a chance on my book! I'd love to read your thoughts on Amazon, Goodreads, Bookbub. Even a line or two of feedback makes all the difference to us authors.

Do you love free stories? Visit my website, www.byrdnash.com and find your next magical read.